THE
GENERAL'S
DEN

THE GENERAL'S DEN

PETER HUBIN

Published by Up North Storytellers

THE GENERAL'S DEN

AN AMAZING DISCOVERY IN THE FOREST

PETER HUBIN

Published by: Up North Storytellers
N4880 Wind Rd., Spooner, WI 54801

Library of Congress Control No. 2010924107

ISBN NO. 978-0-615-35873-4

Printed in the United States of America
By: White Birch Printing, Inc.
501 W. Beaver Brook Ave., Spooner, WI 54801

THE GENERAL'S DEN is fiction with some real time events interspersed with fictional events. The discovery of a door in the forest takes the reader to long ago times and far away places. The story involves a Civil War General.

PREFACE

In the past several years, my wife, Betty, and I have written about our lives and some events in the history of our families. What we remembered about our parents, grandparents and others we put in story form and made a several hundred page booklet to give to each of our children and our grandchildren.

Both of our families have extensive genealogy that go back into the 1500s and we are thankful for that. Our goal was to provide a family history that related to the times and conditions that existed in times past.

In recent years, I have been requested to write about events on my family in our neighborhood of Beaver Brook near Spooner and Shell Lake, Wisconsin. One day Betty said, "You should write a book." The following pages are the result of that suggestion. Thanks to Betty for the suggestion and the many hours typing and retyping this effort on her computer.

There are many things in this story that are true. Most of the story is loosely based on facts, but it is fiction. I leave it up to the reader to separate fact from fiction.

THE GENERAL'S DEN

Chapter 1

~~~~~

Late April, in Northwest Wisconsin, is a time when winter is becoming a distant memory and summer seems just around the corner. My wife, Betty, and I live on a farm and raise beef cattle. April is when most of the calves are born so it is a busy time of the year. Also field work is starting as alfalfa needs to be planted and after that corn, for silage, goes into the ground.

Betty is the treasurer for our township and was at a meeting on the second Tuesday in April. A car pulls into our yard and the driver tells me those dreaded words, "Your cows are out!" Sure enough, ten yearling black angus heifers, in a five acre pasture between our buildings and a busy state highway, had gotten out. These ten heifers were constantly 'roughhousing' with each other, butting heads and generally pushing each other similar to juvenile kids. Apparently they knocked down an electric fence and found a place where the line fence was down.

I fed these heifers grain morning and night, so

I took two pails with grain and ran to where the heifers were out. They were right by the highway. These heifers were a little tempted with the grain, but by now other people stopped and tried to help. The heifers were getting into the excitement of the event by now. Away they went!!! Right through my neighbors yard and bang! Right through the fence and into our main pasture. This should have been fine, except that the group got split in half, with five staying in the pasture, but the other five plowed through a brand new fence and into the woods. They continued on and plowed through our line fence like a runaway freight train. This was very bad news as this is county forest land and is about 4,000 acres in size.

By this time, it was nearly dark so there was nothing we could do anymore that night. The next morning, I was able to get the five heifers that stayed behind confined with some cows that already had baby calves.

I followed the tracks of the five vagabonds. They ran for about a mile before they began to mill around. As I followed their trail, I was reminded of my neighbor, Ed and his Holstein heifers. On July 1st of the year before, timber wolves chased 22 of Ed's heifers out of their pasture. They ran 5 miles on roads and ended up in my neighbors yard at 1:00 a.m. The sheriff was called and my grandson and a friend came to help. They were able to get them into our pasture. My wife and I were out of town and arrived home by noon. Several people were assembled to try to get these heifers into our barnyard. No chance! These heifers broke through my line fence into the vast county forest. It took Ed until the middle of September to finally catch these animals and return them to his farm. That was 2 ½ months full of anxiety and hard work getting feed to these animals deep in the county forest. I am fearful the same fate is in store for me.

Back to my heifers. I eventually lost their trail and returned home. My son and grandson took 4-wheelers and followed snowmobile trails. No luck. Next we contacted a pilot to see if we could find them. The trees were not leafed out yet so we should be able to see them. The pilot and my grandson found the five vagabonds. I took a pail of feed on my 4-wheeler to where they were. When they saw me they ran south, away from home. I went home and took my pick-up to the south end of this huge forest. I followed a logging road and had gone only a short distance and there they were - 2 ½ miles from home. I went home and got some feed. They ate it that evening and again the next morning, but then they disappeared.

The next few days, we looked for them to no avail. Betty and I were celebrating our 50th wedding anniversary in May and had a nice two week trip to Ireland and England planned, starting May 9th. The corn had to be planted and the broken fence needed to be replaced.

One day, I had Betty drop me off on the west side of this huge block of county forest land. I searched on foot and immediately found tracks of one heifer. So apparently there were now four of these 700 pound beauties in one group, and one lonesome one by itself.

I could not follow that single track, so I continued to a small lake thinking the group would need to drink. Hooray! I found a lot of tracks on the shore of the lake. I followed them southeast. They milled around and I could not find their tracks, but I continued in the direction they were heading and it led me to a valley I had never seen before. We have lived at our farm for 37 years and I have hunted and tramped over a large portion of the huge tract of this forest.

I stopped and studied this valley. There was a spring that produced a small stream that flowed into the lake the heifers had traipsed around. Also, there were three small beaver dams on this small stream. On our searches, we saw a lot of timber wolf tracks, many were fresh. I had no weapon and this valley looked imposing. There was a lot of brush near the stream.

I started into the valley and crossed the stream on one of the beaver dams. I found a steep bank blocking my path. I started up the bank and there behind the brush was a DOOR!! It was a wooden door with a latch. It appeared to be about three feet high and three feet wide. I could touch it, but heavy brush and sapling growth prevented me from trying to open it. WOW!!! What was behind that door? Who made it? And how long ago?

The entire huge county forest had all been owned by private citizens including some logging companies. By the 1930s, the Depression forced many land owners to forfeit their property as they could not pay their taxes. This must have been one of those people, or was it?

After pondering my discovery, I continued my search for the heifers. This took me toward another lake. I had not gone more than 400 yards from the door when I came to a rectangular hole in the ground. It had sloping sides, but I could see it had been a basement at one time. Wow, another very interesting discovery. Who? When? Why?

As I searched for my heifers, I could not get my recent discoveries out of my mind. What was behind that door? I made up my mind to go back when I could and open that door. For now though, I had other pressing things to do, like find those heifers and get them back home. They were not only worth about $1,000 each as selected breeding stock to replace older cows in our herd, there is also a possible liability should they cause an accident or cause damage.

Finally, we hired the airplane again, and my grandson, Dexter, and I drove to the small airstrip where the plane was to meet us. As we were walking to the plane, my grandson got a call from one of his friends who was riding his 4-wheeler in our pasture. He is asking, "Why are those cows standing outside the fence?" Dexter said, "Grandpa, go home, the heifers are by the gate going to Jerry's 40 acres." That was great news.

I headed for home, got Betty and a bolt cutter,

plus a pail of feed. We took the tractor back toward the gate and there they were!!

I drove near the gate, cut the chain and opened the gate up. The four beauties were about 80 yards away and just watched me. I poured out a small amount of grain and called them. They came! I moved through the gate and poured out some more. They followed!! I walked behind them and closed the gate. We had them home.

Betty and I were unbelievably happy. Now we could go to Ireland without a cloud hanging over our heads. Granted, there was one gal still missing, but close enough for now. Actually, two days later she found her way back to the herd and jumped over the fence and got back with her pals. WHEW!!! What a relief.

We went to Ireland, rented a car and drove around southern and western Ireland. We had a great time. We also flew to London, rented a car and drove to Stonehenge and Bath. We took a train from the Gatwick Airport into London and toured that beautiful city on the double-decker buses. All in all, we had a wonderful trip. We got back home just a few days before we were to start making hay.

Chapter 2

~~~~~

Now for the door! I took a saw, shovel, crowbar and flashlight and headed off. It was about 1.25 miles from home. I could ride my 4-wheeler to about half mile of the door. Man, I was excited.

I got to the door and cut brush and saplings away. Just enough to get at the door. It had a sliding latch that could work from either side of the door. It was stuck, so I put the crowbar under the door and pried. The latch opened and the door swung inward. I immediately heard a humming sound - what was that? It was low pitched and steady. I turned on my flashlight and looked in. WOW!!

There was a room behind that door. I just looked without going in. The room was dominated by a large stone fireplace in the center of the room. The room was about 16 feet in diameter and was mostly circular. There appeared to be a ledge protruding from one corner of the fireplace. A bench sat near the ledge. Was this a table? There were various pans and dishes around or on the fireplace. There were candle holders on the fireplace also.

The walls were made out of rocks mortared

together. The ceiling was made of huge oak timbers with one end resting on the stone walls of the side of the den and the other end resting on the fireplace, which was higher than the walls. Some type of heavy boards rested on the big timbers. I withdrew from the doorway and went looking for the roof of this - this DEN?

What I found when I climbed up were small trees and brush growing around a hole in the ground. The hole was the flue for the fireplace. Whoever built this must have first dug a hole and then began laying the rocks for the walls. Judging by the number and size of these rocks, it would have been a major project to find and haul these rocks. It would have taken several workers a fairly long time to build the walls and the fireplace. The roof was then covered with dirt so vegetation could grow there.

I went back to the doorway. Was it safe inside? My light shining on the big timbers showed some type of tar like paper over the top. The timbers appeared to be very solid. Perhaps I could go in the den. A few hooks were attached to the timbers.

The door did not go all the way to the floor. I eased over the door casing and had to step down about 2 ½ feet to reach the dirt floor. Interesting! Now I could see what was on the other side of the fireplace.

Slowly, I cautiously moved a step. What was that humming? Where was it coming from? Finally, I could see the wall that had been blocked by the fireplace. There was an opening in the wall and a tunnel led away from the wall.

I take one or two more steps and look at the backside of the fireplace. Wow! There was a bed of sorts and there was the **remains of a man laying on that bed!** The bed was part of the fireplace and was actually a bench made out of stones with a frame of wood and branches on top of the bench. The man had been dead for a very long time, maybe 50 to 100 years or more.

The man was lying on his back. His flesh was all dried up and his skin was stretched over his bones. He appeared to be mummified. There were some blankets over his lower body. He was wearing a shirt that appeared to be made of animal skin of some sort. The man seemed of ordinary size, certainly not very large. It appears as if he just laid down and died, maybe in his sleep.

I was getting nervous. The humming continued. I flashed the light around the room. Above the bed was a gun held up by pegs put into the fireplace. It was a lever action with an octagon barrel. That baby was old. I did not touch it.

I looked under the bed and there was an opening. I positioned myself to be able to look into the opening. Further in the opening there was a metal box. What was in that box? I did not touch that either.

This was quite the discovery. I needed to look in that tunnel. I got in front of the tunnel and shined my light in. It was not lined and was about 3 feet in diameter. It went about 15 feet and then curved to the right. I could not see the end of the tunnel. There were some tools leaning up against the wall, or laying down on the edge of the tunnel. I could see a shovel, axe, adze, crosscut saw, hammers and other tools not entirely visible. Also hanging on one side, in a little indent, were many traps of various sizes. This was curious because the main room had no tools, just pots, pans, dishes, silverware, several pencils and many knives. I wondered where extra clothes were, if any. I walked to the other end of the fireplace and, low and behold, it was a closet of sorts. Clothes were hanging there, as were some clothes on a shelf in the lower part of the closet. Two pair of boots sat on the floor.

I did not touch anything other than the door to get in. What an amazing discovery! I decided to leave and come back after I sorted out things in my mind. After all, this was on county property and a dead person was found. This could get to be a sticky wicket.

Chapter 3

~~~~~

On the way home, many questions popped into my head. Why was that location chosen? When? What did this man eat? Were there other family members? Was that property his, or was he a squatter? Did he hunt? Fish? Cut lumber? How did he get supplies, and why did he come here?

I was hopeful that many answers may be in the metal box under the bed. Arriving home, I related to Betty what I had discovered. She agreed, "We need to keep this to ourselves until we know many answers." We both were astounded by the fact that the man had lived there and no one had discovered his den until now. We also vowed not to harm it in anyway. After all, it was not our property and a dead man was involved. It was easy to see a lot of legal issues could lie ahead.

I had made up my mind to return to the den and open that metal box. Making hay was underway, but I knew a rainy day would come along. I could hardly wait.

Finally, I could return to the den. Betty came with me. We opened the door and eased into the den. Immediately, the humming started. Betty was as amazed as I was when I first saw it. Betty looked around, but I went right to the metal box. I pulled it out and put it on the shelf of the fireplace. We opened the box and saw its contents seemed in good condition. We immediately saw many pages of paper, or pages made out of skins. Along one side of the box were some coins. They appeared to be gold. Also near the coins was a large compass. There was part of a box of .44 caliber rim fire shells and a partial box of 10 gauge shotgun shells. We carefully lifted the sheets of paper, which seemed to be some sort of a diary. There were two letters next, and a few receipts for supplies. At the bottom of the box was an official looking document. We carefully opened it and saw it was a patent for this property. This document showed how the land went from public ownership by the government to private ownership.

This patent was made to Benjamin G. Mason, Blue Ridge Summit, Pennsylvania. Forty acres was given to Benjamin for fighting in the Indian Wars under 'Captain Billy'. The description of the land was in Wisconsin, NE 40A of the SW Section 12, Township 38N, Range 12W. It was drafted on April 15, 1839 AD. It was signed by the President of the United States, Martin Van Buren.

So, apparently Benjamin received this 40A as part of his pay for fighting in the Indian Wars. I know that other land got 'deeded over' in this manner for other reasons, some for fighting in the Civil War and other military service. Also, homesteading was done and a patent for the land was awarded when requirements were met, always signed by the President of the United States.

My guess is that the dead man was Benjamin G. Mason. Strange that today this land belongs to the county, so when Benjamin failed to pay his taxes, the county took over the property. I wonder what year. Who did Benjamin pay taxes to, if he came here around 1840? But then again, the patent shows he was awarded the land in 1839. It does not mean he came here straight away. Maybe those other papers will tell when Benjamin came to this land. I know that this part of Wisconsin was surveyed in 1855. Perhaps some surveying was done before that.

As we would not remove anything from the den, we were in a quandary. After much discussion, we decided to leave the coins, compass and shells but take the other papers home, make copies and then return them to the den.

I decided to crawl into the tunnel to at least see around the bend. This was scary! In I went. My light revealed that the tunnel continued to curve to the right. I could not see an end to it, so I backed out. That tunnel was mysterious.

I shined the light under the bed to see if anything was there besides the box. Yes, there was a pile of steel strips. I pulled it out and realized that the strips were all connected and I recognized it as a 'surveyor chain'. This discovery, along with the compass, told me that Benjamin was a surveyor, or had been at one time.

Before leaving the den with the metal box, we looked around. There was no animal damage and no structural damage. I noticed a flue handle on the front of the fireplace. It appeared to be closed. This would keep animals from coming down the chimney. Certainly squirrels, raccoons, mice and chipmunks would explore any opening like a chimney flue. Also, just inside the opening to the tunnel was a collection of rocks. Ah, ha! Those rocks could be used to seal off the tunnel if Benjamin had to retreat into the tunnel. Maybe the tunnel was a safe room, or maybe an escape route if attack of some kind occurred. We will have to go back in the tunnel, but not today.

We headed for home, anxious to see what the papers in the box had to say. Also on our mind, was when did this occur? Another thought crossing our mind, fleetingly, what happens to the remains of the man we presume to be Benjamin G. Mason? Will he be buried somewhere? If so, where? Should his death be investigated, like a very old cold case? Who would do that? What is our role in all of this? Are we criminals for tampering with a crime scene? It is beginning to look like this discovery has plenty of slippery slope around it. We better be super careful and keep our mouths shut until we see a clear path in dealing with Benjamin.

We got the box home and opened it. Besides the patent, we found many pages of what appeared to be a log or diary. Also there were two envelopes addressed to Benjamin in Blue Ridge Summit, Pennsylvania. There was no return address and no postmark.

We made copies of the letters and the other papers. One paper stood out as not part of the diary. It was a sketch of a piece of property, perhaps the land the den was on. It showed four corner posts and a dotted line connecting a faraway point. It showed compass headings starting at a point that was not legible. It went

North 1320 ft., West 1320 ft., South 1320 ft. and East 1320 ft.

There was a wavy line running NW to SE and it started near the SE corner of this 40 acre property. Also shown was a circle on the east side of the wavy line. Was it the location of the den?

Back to the envelopes. We opened one and it was very fragile. It was dated August 12, 1865 and was signed by a Lucy, no last name. The other letter was also from Lucy and was dated September 4, 1865.

The first letter to Benjamin told him that her brothers were beginning to return from the war. She hoped they would not come after Benjamin, but he better be on the watch. Signed: Love, Lucy.

The next letter of September 4, 1865 warned Benjamin that her brothers had returned to Hagerstown and were upset about things that happened in the war. She told Benjamin that he should consider leaving. She said she loved him, but she feared for his life. She signed it: Love forever, Lucy.

With no postmark, or return address, it must have been delivered by someone - not a mailman. So apparently there was bad blood between Benjamin and Lucy's brothers. Blue Ridge Summit is in Pennsylvania which was a northern state. Just across the border is Hagerstown, Maryland, a southern state, and that is where Lucy said her brothers were returning. The light comes on! The Mason-Dixon Line separates these two states and forms the border between the north and south, in that part of the United States.

I think that Benjamin G. Mason was a surveyor. Could he have been the Mason of Mason-Dixon? A quick Google on the internet showed the Mason-Dixon Line was surveyed between 1763 and 1767. That Mason was Charles. This line is marked by tall stones every mile. These stones were imported from England and the Maryland side is marked with an M and the Pennsylvania side is marked with a P. Mason & Dixon also are engraved on the stones.

Benjamin G. Mason may have worked on the line at a later date. He may, or may not, have been related to Charles Mason. At any rate, we know why he left Blue Ridge Summit, Pennsylvania. We don't know when.

Back to the many pages of the diary. The papers were somewhat difficult to read. Benjamin's hand writing was somewhat hard to read. Also, very few dates were recorded. We made copies and then began to read Benjamin's story.

We tried to figure out how old Benjamin was at the end of the war. He received the patent from President Van Buren   dated April 15, 1839. This was for his service during the Indian Wars. Benjamin could have been as young as 16 in 1839. By the end of the Civil War, he could be about 42 years old, or older. So, by the time Benjamin got to his land, he could have been 42, or older. He did mention taking trains, and Wausau, Wisconsin was also mentioned. Railroads finally came to this part of Wisconsin in 1879. Very likely Benjamin either walked or rode a horse, or had a horse and wagon to get from Wausau to his land. Wausau is about 125 miles toward the southeast from here.

In 1865, there were no main roads in this area. The land was surveyed in 1855 so some markers were established. Benjamin, being a surveyor, probably knew where and how to look for existing markers. With no roads, this would have been very slow going.

One of the early entries tells of finally finding his property. That entry was dated June 1866. *It took him several days to measure out the 40 acres. He made four stakes out of red oak. He whittled all the bark off and made them four sided. He next carved his name on two sides. He then put them in a fire to char them. He made sure the charcoal was uniform all over the stakes. He then went to the corners of his property and pounded the stakes in. This marked his property and because of the charcoal, the stakes may be there yet. I will look for them later.*

Benjamin looked over his property. There was a small spring near the southeast corner. There was a Beaver dam and pond downstream. The stream ran into a lake about half mile from the spring. The 40 acres had beautiful red oak, white oak, maple, basswood, ash, white birch, cherry, elm and aspen. He commented that there is plenty of wood to build a cabin. He noted that there were plenty of rocks near the stream.

Another entry sounded an alarm. *He saw several people going toward the lake. Indians!! Now he was concerned. He did not know if they were dangerous. He wrote that from now on he must not call attention to himself. No fires except at night, don't leave tracks, keep sounds to a minimum, keep rifle handy and be careful.*

Next entry tells that he begins digging to make a hole to serve as his home. He must have found some way to carry the dirt away. He decided to try to catch some fish in the lake. He found angle worms and apparently had fish line and hooks. He was careful to not leave tracks. He wrote: *caught a large pike. Enough for several days meals. Dried some.*

Benjamin started placing rocks. He found a clay pocket that he could mix with sand to make a kind of mortar to hold the rocks in place. He noted that he could hear wolves howling and once found their tracks where he was working on the rocks. He also saw an elk. His den was about 15 feet from the stream and 75 feet from the spring. He had dug out the spring and if he could find a container he could keep food cool by putting it in the spring.

Next entry: *Got the stone work done. Selected large white oak for roof. Began cutting oaks.* He cut them to proper length using the crosscut saw. He peeled the bark off and used his adze to shape them into four sided beams. He built a ramp affair to push the heavy beams in place.

Next entry, dated August 1866. *Got the beams all in place. Cut white oak trees to place over the beams. Used adze to square up and remove bark. Took several days. Began cutting to length and placing on the big beams. Put down tarred paper on beams first.*

Next entry - no date: *Shoveled dirt on roof of structure. Cut white oak to make a door. Started fire in fireplace and it worked. Saw a large bear near stream.*

Next entry, dated September 1866. *Saw several Indians. Came from the east in a single file and went to the lake. I counted eight. No children. Stayed by lake for the night. No fire tonight for Benjamin. The Indians were hunting geese and catching fish. Stayed all day and night. Left in morning. They went west in single file. Must be careful. They all carried weapons.*

Next entry - no date: *Gathered wood for fire. Worked on tunnel. Shot a deer. Dried meat. Tanned hide and will make jacket and shirt. Heard geese on lake. Sneaked up and shot two.*

Next entry, December, 1866: *Lots of snow. Must be careful not to leave any more tracks than needed.*

Next entry, Summer of 1867. *No sign of Lucy's brothers. Traps have been set.*

Chapter 4

~~~~~

WOW! Have traps set! What does he mean? I wonder why Benjamin thinks Lucy's brothers would come from Hagerstown, Maryland to track him down in Northern Wisconsin. How would they find him? Did he tell Lucy where he was going?

If he left Blue Ridge Summit in 1865 and didn't show up at his land until 1866, he must have gone other places before coming here. Or he took a long time to get here.

From the little bit we know about Benjamin, it was hard to guess how Lucy's brothers would know where to look. Ah, ha! The patent! Perhaps they know about this patent of 1839 giving 40 acres to Benjamin. With some inquiry, they could have found the survey coordinates for Benjamin's 40 acres. They would have a serious reason to search for Benjamin half way across the United States. I wonder what the reason is.

My guess is it is like the Hatfield's and McCoy's which was a huge family feud over the Civil War. Benjamin lived in a northern state and fought for the north apparently. Lucy's brothers lived in a southern state and apparently fought for the south. Maybe there was a big feud between the families! Maybe they fought against each other in big battles like Gettysburg or Antietam or Vicksburg.

Chapter 5

~~~~~

My work on the farm was picking up. We finally got nice weather and with 200 acres of hay to put up, I got busy and finished the first crop. About the time I got the haying done, the big rodeo comes to town. Betty and I have worked on this for many years, so about a week of our life gets devoted to it each year.

Back to haying. This involves many hours of driving tractor. First cutting with a discbine, then when it is dry, raking it into windrows and then baling it into large round bales. In a few days, the bales are loaded on to wagons and hauled home to put in big barns.

All this tractor time gives me plenty of time to think. Such as: Apparently when Benjamin died it wasn't during the cold weather because the damper on his fireplace was closed. Apparently it was summertime, or spring or fall. Benjamin would not need much heat during this time. The den was small and underground. A fire at night would probably keep the den nice and warm. It would have been dark except near the fire. Candles were used. Benjamin must have lived on meat from deer, geese, fish and maybe elk or bear. Benjamin must have been good at drying this meat in order to keep it from spoiling. Getting a large animal like a deer, elk or bear would need to be harvested in the winter so cold weather would preserve the meat. Bears hibernate in winter, but maybe a den could be found. Today there are large numbers of bear in this area.

I wonder if a meat or fish diet would eventually lead to health problems. Benjamin could find raspberries, blueberries, blackberries, choke cherries, and pin cherries in the summer. Depending on the year, hazel nuts may be found. In the fall, cranberries may have been available as well as wild rice.

The Indians Benjamin saw would be seeking these same berries, nuts and rice. Without a canoe or boat, wild rice would be very difficult to harvest. Today there is no wild rice within a few miles of Benjamin's den. Benjamin would have to be very wary not to be detected by the Indians he had seen earlier. He was not sure if they were hostile or not.

The paper Benjamin wrote on was strange. Perhaps it wasn't paper at all. It may have been animal skin. At any rate, after a few pages the words were very difficult to read, sometimes impossible to read. Perhaps we need to find someone that can make the words readable. That means someone else will know about Benjamin. We better check the internet and perhaps we can make the missing words readable.

Chapter 6

~~~~~

Benjamin had stated that the traps were set. This got me thinking. We found 10 gauge shotgun shells in the metal box, but we did not find a shotgun. Could that gun have been rigged with a trip cord to protect Benjamin from Indians? Perhaps the brothers that Lucy talked about in Hagerstown would try to find him in Wisconsin.

How would he rig a shotgun to do this? Where would it be set up? Thinking of the area around the den, I thought the most logical way to approach the den would be along the stream. I needed to get back to the den with my metal detector and look for that shotgun. If the gun is indeed there, it may still be loaded. This could be dangerous.

I was finally able to return to the den and search for a possible 'booby trapped' shotgun. I had my metal detector, pry bar and flashlight. This would be my third visit to Benjamin's den.

I approached the den from the down stream side, which means I was moving toward the southeast. As I got close, I moved carefully!!! I was using the metal detector, but looking for any possible set up for a shotgun and looking for any wire or other devices that might trigger a shotgun blast.

Thinking backward to the 1860s, well over 135 years ago, I realized that the landscape may be nearly the same, but trees and vegetation would have changed over and over again in that length of time.

I moved carefully as I got near the den. I swept the metal detector in a wide area. No sign of the shotgun as I neared the den. I backtracked and took a new path up on the bank, or on a level with the den's roof. This route was still in a southeasterly direction.

As I carefully moved along, I tried to picture this terrain as it was 135 years ago. Perhaps big white pine grew here. After all, that is what brought the lumberjacks to northwest Wisconsin. Big outfits like Knapp, Stout and Dunn may have logged here. The Shell Lake Lumber Company owned by J. J. Bourne owned land in this area.

I swept the metal detector as I moved toward the den. That sweep was unproductive, so I returned and began a new sweep further away from the stream, but parallel to it. All of a sudden the metal detector beeped and beeped!! I swept the area and the detector beeped like crazy.

I carefully started pulling leaves and debris away. After several minutes my hand felt a steel barrel. It was a shotgun! It was a double barreled shotgun and both hammers were cocked!

I carefully cleared the material away to reveal the entire gun. I looked at the triggers to try to detect any kind of triggering set up as a booby trapped gun would have.

There were several copper rivets near the trigger guard. Perhaps some kind of leather device was riveted together that would fire the gun. What kind of material was to actually trip that gun? It could have been deer or elk skin made into a long string. It could have been stretched tightly so when some one, or something, moved into the string it would fire one, or both barrels of the 10 gauge shotgun. At 20 to 40 feet that would be a deadly blast.

The gun was aimed at a spot on the east side of the stream and about 30 feet away from the end of the gun barrel. If it was set to shoot a man it would have hit him near the chest.

Why was the gun still cocked? Maybe the string

rotted away. Maybe it was visible and could be detected. Maybe no large animal or man passed on the path to trip the gun. At any rate, both hammers were cocked.

I stepped back and thought long and hard for awhile. Could this gun be booby trapped so if someone picked it up it would trigger another gun somewhere? Perhaps it might be rigged up to dynamite. After 135 or so years, nothing may work, but then again, it may still work. I was not anxious to take that chance.

Perhaps I could find a long dead sapling and use it to push the gun out of its bed. I began searching for a sapling, but I swept the pathway in front of me with the metal detector. I did find a dead sapling on the ground. It was about 20 feet long and I could just manage to pick it up and bring it back to the shotgun. I put the small end up against the gun and nudged it. Nothing happened. I nudged it again and pushed it out of its bed. Still nothing happened. I put the sapling down and picked up my metal detector and swept the area around and under where the gun rested. No new beeps, so I put down the detector and picked up the shotgun.

The gun was severely rusted. I tried to un-cock

the hammers, but they would not release. I tried to open the gun, but it was rusted so badly that it would not open. Now what? There probably are two live 10 gauge shotgun shells in the chamber. If the hammers won't release, I don't think it could fire, but I am not certain.

I tried to see what brand of shotgun it was, but rusting had made that impossible for now. It had to be a least 135 years old and maybe older. Its style was certainly old fashioned compared to today's shotguns.

What should I do now? The gun was not mine so I can't take it home and try to clean it up. It didn't seem to bother me to take the metal box home to copy pages. I will return it, but for now I have taken something that is not mine from property that is not mine. I am probably in hot water right now. Would the water be any hotter if I took the gun home, tried to clean it and bring it back? Another view is 'finders keepers, losers weepers.' I don't think so.

I tried to weigh all arguments. I don't think I should return it to the spot I found it. Perhaps it was a murder weapon. Maybe a murder weapon more than once. Talk about a cold case, very cold. I really did not want to take the gun home even if I planned to return it. I did not think that now was the time to talk to the County Forest Administrator. I am pretty sure that it will occur sometime, but in the mean time there are way too many questions that don't have answers. In the end, I thought my best plan would be to put the rusted shotgun in Benjamin's den and hope it did not go off and hurt someone.

Chapter 7

~~~~~

Benjamin had written that the traps were set. That would imply that there were at least two traps and maybe more. Since that was written in the summer I am thinking he was not trapping animals for their fur. Did Benjamin have another shotgun rigged with a trip wire? Or was it another type of trap? If so, what was it and where was it set?

Undoubtedly this, or these, traps must be near the den. Benjamin was apparently afraid of the Indians, or was it Lucy's brothers from Maryland. It would seem that Benjamin could write or telegraph Lucy, but in the 1860s or '70s in Northern Wisconsin, the telegraph was not close by yet. I don't know how far Benjamin would have to go to mail a letter. Besides, it would have a postmark that might give away his location. So might sending a telegraph. Apparently Benjamin must have reason to think they will track him down and settle what ever grudge is between them. It must be serious stuff.

I took the shotgun to the den door, pried it up and pushed it open, turned on my flashlight and started in with the shot gun. Immediately the humming started. What was that? Was it real or was it some ghostly sound connected with Benjamin's death?

At any rate, I took the shotgun into the den and looked for a place to put it that was safe. I looked at the lever action rifle, resting on stone pegs in the back of the fireplace. Low and behold, below the rifle were two pegs built into the fireplace. Perhaps this was the shotguns home before it was pressed into duty as an agent of ambush. I put the shotgun on the pegs. I stepped back and looked at the remains of Benjamin G. Mason, the mystery man from Blue Ridge Summit, Pennsylvania.

His life in the den must have been dull. There were no visitors, apparently. He led a life of nearly complete isolation. He had a very limited food diet. The den would have been dark except for candles, light from the fire and when the door was opened. Benjamin probably did not know when Christmas was or any other holiday. Benjamin really must have feared for his life. He must have been a master at concealing his movements, not leaving tracks, fire smoke, wood gathering, searching for food and just exploring the surrounding rolling woodlands and later running a trap line to catch fur bearers. I looked around the den, marveling at its construction. The eight heavy beams that rested one end on the stone wall and the other on the fire place appeared to be very strong, yet remnants of skin strings still dangled from some of the beams. What had hung there? Perhaps herbs were gathered and dried to be used if Benjamin was sick. Which, by the way, Benjamin had no medical help anywhere nearby. What did he die from? Old age? Was he sick? Had he been wounded in a fight with someone, or something like a bear or a cougar? Had he suffered from Alzheimer's disease.

Just on a whim, I brought the metal detector into the den. I started sweeping the dirt floor. I picked up beeps in several places. What was down there? Since I didn't have a shovel, I would have to search the floor on another trip. Later, I realized I could have used Benjamin's shovel.

I began sweeping the walls, not expecting anything behind or in the stone wall. Immediately, I picked up beeping on the north side of the den, about 3 feet off the floor. I put the light on the spot and noticed the mortar was somewhat different around three or four stones. I picked at the mortar and it fell out. I was able to take one rock out and then another.

At first I could not see anything, but then I noticed the corner of a small metal box. I loosened up another stone and then I could see most of a small metal box. I reached in and lifted the box out. It was very heavy and was about eight inches long, five inches wide and three inches deep. It had a clasp, but no lock on it. I put the box on the flat stone of the fire place. What was in this box?

Chapter 8

~~~~~

I opened the box which was nearly full. On top were several United States Dollars. These were very fragile, but I could see the word gold on a couple of them. Below the paper currency were several gold coins and several silver coins.

Below the money was a folded up document type paper. I carefully lifted it out and opened it. About half of it was torn off and was missing. It was some sort of Discharge Document from the Civil War! The way the paper was torn made it difficult to read what it had to tell. Besides, the paper had disintegrated and some of the writing was so diminished that it was nearly impossible to read.

What I could read started with the soldiers name, which was BENJAM, the rest of the name was missing. Was it Benjamin G. Mason? Next some wording apparently praising his service in the United States Army. Once again many words were missing or indistinguishable. Next was a part that described the unit he was assigned to. It was the Pennsylvania 6. The torn off part contained the rest of his units number. He saw service in the Wilder and at Vi. The missing paper may have been able to complete Wilderness and Vicksburg. Just a guess.

Finally, the soldier was discharged with the rank of Brigadier Gen and the date was April 4, 18 . Once again, the torn paper may have contained the letters to spell out General. Perhaps Benjamin G. Mason was a Civil War General! I guess I immediately thought that was the case. Maybe that was an incorrect supposition.

Why was this document torn? Was the other missing part in the den somewhere? Had someone else torn it out of spite? Where else did Benjamin serve? Undoubtedly he had to send his troops into harms way on many occasions during that bloody war. Could a disgruntled former soldier of Benjamin's somehow been able to rip the document? Had Benjamin been leading his troops against forces from Maryland that could have had Lucy's brothers in it? If so, had Benjamin's actions been such that it placed the Maryland soldiers at a severe handicap, or perhaps got them trapped and they were either killed or captured. Maybe that was it. Benjamin's troops may have captured Lucy's brothers and maybe they are relatives of Benjamin. Wouldn't that be a terrible thing. Having to surrender to a family relative? Maybe that did not happen. Maybe it did. We will have to check Civil War records to see if there is any evidence to support any theory.

I went back to looking into the box. I looked to see if it had a false bottom. It did not seem like it. The box contained a fair amount of currency and coin, but not a fortune. I went back to the hole in the rocks. Was there any thing else there? My light and hand could not detect anything. How about the metal detector. I put it in the hole and it beeped. Something metal was still in the hole or nearby. About then my flashlight got very dim. I gathered up the metal box, Discharge Document, the metal detector and left the den. I closed the door and looked around. The door opened to the southwest, the spring was to my left, or to the southeast. The lake was to my right, or to the northwest. I still had some daylight so I tried to figure out what other trap Benjamin may have set. I don't think it was another booby trapped gun, as no other ammunition besides the .44 caliber and 10 gauge were found. Perhaps it was a deep hole that was covered over that someone could fall into.

The gun was set up to get someone coming from the northwest. Perhaps the other trap was to get someone coming from the southeast

Chapter 9

~~~~~

I had walked from the spring to the den a couple of times and certainly did not find a hole, or anything that resembled a hole. However, there was a tree that had recently fallen near the spring. It was a large white oak with many limbs. I had to go around the tree. Perhaps the hole may be under the tree! I took the metal detector and started into the treetop. I swept with the metal detector just in case there was another gun booby trap, or some other metal trap. After fighting my way into about the center of the downed tree top, the metal detector beeped! What was it?

I continued sweeping with the metal detector and it beeped in the same place. Something metal was there and it was under a giant limb. I got down on all fours and started looking closely at the ground. I reached over the limb and felt the ground. There wasn't anything! There was just a big hole!

I went back out and approached the tree from the other side. I made my way in using the metal detector. As I got near the hole, the detector beeped. Whatever was metal was in the hole. Finally, I got in far enough so I could see the hole. It was about 3 feet in diameter. Without the flashlight I could not see the bottom. I crawled out and got my flashlight. Hopefully it would have enough power to at least look to see if I could see the bottom.

I crawled back in and got into position so I could see down into the hole. I turned on the light. Holy Cow! There was a human skull impaled on a bayonet! The light completely failed so I was done here, for now.

I took the small metal box with me and headed for home. Betty is going to be surprised at what I found today. I still am wondering about the humming. It is spooky.

On my way to the four wheeler, I walk near the rectangular hole in the ground located about 400 yards from the den. I stop and take the metal detector and start sweeping. It beeps several times on the edge of the hole. Perhaps these were nails. Down in the hole, which was largely V shaped, the detector beeped and beeped. Something metal was there and seemed to be in great abundance. What was it? What was this building site anyway? Another mystery.

I showed Betty the Discharge Document and the money when I got home. I told her about the light going dim as I got strong beeps from the metal detector in the hole where the box was located. I plugged in the flashlight so it would be ready tomorrow.

Chapter 10

~~~~~

Our minds were working overtime. Where could we find out more about Benjamin's service record during the Civil War. Betty would search the internet and I would go to the library.

That research would probably take time, but in the meanwhile, I needed to find a way to see what was written on the papers, or animal skins, found in the first box. It was funny that the papers on the top were mostly legible. The paper, or skins, under the top three sheets were not readable, except for a word or letter here and there.

I got out several sheets. There were nine that were unreadable. I tried shining a light from the side and presto! Many of the depressions made as the words were put on the paper showed up. More than half of the pages were mostly readable.

Next I wrote down what I could read of each page. I then took a fluorescent light and shown it on the paper. No luck. Then I held the light behind the paper. Bulls-eye! More words were visible but still about a quarter of the words were not clear.

The pages were in no particular order. I looked at the pages I had made by using both lights. Very few dates were listed. I found where Benjamin wrote about two intruders being killed by his traps. That was all that was said. Were they Lucy's brothers?

No emotion about someone being blasted by two barrels of a 10 gauge shotgun. Nothing said about the one who fell in the hole and got skewered by the bayonet. Being a Civil War General, Benjamin probably saw untold deadly scenes. He undoubtedly took part in many deadly battles, some went hand to hand. It must have made him very hard hearted.

A very interesting entry made the summer of 1877. *Heard men's voices today. Saw several men cutting trees, digging a hole in the ground one quarter mile north of me. Built low cabin over the hole in the ground. I must be careful.*

Also entry the fall of 1877. *Several people now live in the cabin. Could be Trading Post. Last night I heard shots and shouting. Cabin is burned down.*

Went to cabin site - several days later. All were dead. Hair scalped off. Three men. Indians did this. Same ones I saw.

Wow! Apparently Benjamin had not been detected by the Indians or the people that built the cabin. If they were traders, who were they going to trade with. I guess the Indians were not all friendly. Perhaps the traders tried to trick the Indians.

Now I am really curious. What made the metal detector beep down in the hole? The Indians would have been able to take anything of value before they burned the cabin. Perhaps something was buried in the floor. I need to bring a shovel - soon.

Benjamin thought the killers were Indians. I wonder what his reasons were. Did he hear war whoops? Did he find arrows? Was there scalping? Anyone can scalp. Maybe we are giving a bad rap to the Indians in the fall of 1877. It does appear that this cabin was built on the pathway the Indians used when they came to the lake to shoot geese and catch pike. Perhaps they didn't want anyone infringing on their hunting and fishing grounds. Looks like local zoning in effect.

Chapter 11

~~~~~

Another entry made the spring of 1878. *Heard train whistle to the southwest. Walked toward it. After nearly three miles I crossed small river. There are trout in it. Finally came to railroad. Men building tunnel out of limestone. Talked to the men. Watched workmen. Large train engine. Had boom to raise big limestone blocks. Asked about telegraph. Closest is at Rice Lake.*

The tunnel Benjamin is talking about is one I am very familiar with as it was only about a quarter mile from the country school I attended the first four years of my schooling. It is a beautiful limestone tunnel about eight feet high and seven feet wide. It goes under the railroad that was built in 1879. That track goes from Eau Claire to Superior or Ashland. The tunnel was well known to the kids in the area. It took a lot of courage to be in the tunnel when a train came over it. It took me a few tries before I stayed in the tunnel when the train came over. To this day, I still marvel at the skill of the tunnel builders and would like to have watched them actually build this tunnel. It is a reminder of a long ago skill and very hard work.

Another entry - *Walked to Rice Lake, traded furs. Got meal, shirts, pants, boots, others. Telegraphed Lucy. Waited. No answer.*

No date on that entry. First try to contact Lucy. Who is she? Wonder if Benjamin and Lucy were sweet on each other before the war, or is she a relative. Perhaps Lucy's brothers were surveyors also. May have worked with Benjamin before the Civil War. Blue Ridge Summit and Hagerstown are only a few miles apart. Maybe at one time Benjamin lived in Hagerstown. Maybe he went from there to fight for Captain Billy during the Indian Wars. He was probably very young, maybe as young as 16 or 17.

What ever - something very bad happened to the relationship to Benjamin and Lucy's brothers apparently during the Civil War. Internet search and library search does not answer any questions. If General Mason's troops did capture Lucy's brothers that would have put Benjamin in a very tough predicament. He could not show preference to Lucy's brothers, or could he have? That is one of the ways that the Civil War is different from other bloody wars our soldiers fought. You may be fighting against your neighbors, or worse yet, your relatives during a civil war. Very sad predicament for any soldier.

Do I shoot someone I know, or one related to me, or do they shoot me? I hope I am never put in that situation. I can almost be sure that something like that happened to Benjamin and Lucy's brothers.

Did Benjamin tip off his location by telegraphing Lucy? Maybe all the brothers are dead? Maybe their sons will continue to search for Benjamin. The quest to 'even the score' can go through several generations. If only we had a last name for Lucy's brothers.

With the flashlight charged up, Betty and I went back to the den. We had a shovel, as well as the pry bar and metal detector. We also had the original box with its papers, or skins, in it. We intended to put the coins, compass and ammunition back in it and return it to its place under Benjamin's bed. That is an armful to carry on the four wheeler, but we managed. We decided to keep the paper/skins at home for now, in hopes of being able to decipher more information from them.

We walked past the hole in the ground where the three people were killed and scalped. We would dig on the way back.

I showed Betty where I found the shotgun. I showed her where the hole was under the downed white oak tree. She declined the offer to creep in and look at the skull with bayonet stuck in it. It was pretty gross.

We went to the door of Benjamin's den, pried the door up and opened it. Immediately the humming started. Was that Benjamin's ghost? I don't believe in ghosts, but that sound is down right ghostly.

We climbed into the den. I showed Betty the rusty 10 gauge shotgun. We go to the hole in the rocks, stick the metal detector in and it beeps. We look in and don't see anything but rocks on all sides and dirt behind it. I started probing with my knife and immediately hit something. I dig a little and see something that is not a rock or dirt. More digging and out comes a gold pocket watch on a chain. It is very tarnished, but I know it will clean up. There appears to be engraving on the back. I can not read it. We will take it home and clean it up. My guess is it belonged to one of the people killed by Benjamin's traps. We put the metal detector back in the hole and it beeps. More digging with my knife and I find another gold watch and chain. It is in the same condition. It needs to be cleaned. We put the detector back in the hole and it beeped again. Is there another watch? More digging with my knife and I find a knife in a belt sheath. Did this belong to one of the watch owners or was it on a third victim of Benjamin's traps? There was no name on either the knife or sheath, but it was very badly corroded.

We use the metal detector and dig where it beeps. We are surprised to find small pieces of native copper. These are pure chunks of copper carried here by the glaciers of 11,000 years ago. We add them to the small metal box.

Chapter 12

~~~~~~

Let's hope that when we clean up those gold watches that there will be names we can read. All the while, there lies Benjamin a few feet from us. It does not bother us, but he makes Betty feel a little uneasy. But Benjamin, old boy, we are slowly learning your story and eventually we tell your story for all the world to know. For now there are too many missing parts. Maybe they will always be missing.

We put the metal detector back in the hole and this time there is no beeping. We put the stones back and start sweeping the rest of the walls. No beeps on the walls. I pause and look at the way Benjamin constructed the door. It does have wooden hinges that work just fine. The door is made of two layers of wood with each layer about 1 ½ inches thick so the door is about 3 inches thick and measures about 3 ½ feet by 3 ½ feet. The layers are held together with wooden pegs. I have not found a brace and bit yet, so there must be one in the den some place.

Apparently Benjamin must have used the adze to make the planks for the door. His saw was a cross cut saw and would not have worked to saw boards. It was hard to tell how the planks were cut, too much weathering and age on them.

I hated to do it, but I felt I must take the metal detector into the tunnel. Perhaps I will find something. I will also go far enough to see where the tunnel leads. Betty went outside to wait since we had only one flashlight.

I started into the tunnel with the metal detector. As I came near the shovel, axe, cross cut saw, adze, hammer and a few small tools like screwdriver, wrenches, and leather scissors all made the metal detector beep like crazy. I moved on into the tunnel, sweeping as I went. There were no beeps from the detector. The tunnel curved to the right and by now I was further along the tunnel than before. Still no beeps. Finally I could see something ahead. It blocked the tunnel, but I could see a tiny bit of light on one side. It was a door!

I crawled up to it and shouted to Betty. She heard me and came to the sound of my voice. I told her it looked like a door. Could she see it from the outside? For a long time she could not see it, but finally she said yes, she could see some boards behind some shrubs. I had put the metal detector down so I crawled back to get it and swept the tunnel up to the door. It beeped near the door. I looked and found the missing brace & bit. What was it doing here? Had Benjamin been working on the door and just left it here? Had he injured himself and left in a hurry to seek out his bed? Maybe that was the last thing Benjamin did before he died. By my calculations, he could have been at least 56, or maybe much older. Perhaps he suffered an attack like a heart attack and was able to get to his bed. There was part of a candle laying near the brace and bit.

The tunnel apparently was built for storage, but also an escape route. The door came out about 50 feet from the den door and was closer to the spring. Perhaps if Benjamin felt he was trapped, he could either escape or get an advantage over an assailant. By now, my flashlight was nearly out of power so I retreated and closed the door, which caused the humming to stop.

Chapter 13

~~~~~

Betty and I went to the large rectangular hole in the ground, located about 400 yards from the den, and did as we planned. We used the metal detector to see what was buried in the ground at the bottom of the hole. Small trees were growing in the hole so digging would be difficult. We started sweeping with the metal detector and found a very strong beep in a definite location. This must be a good place to start.

I started digging. The tree roots made it very hard to work. I had dug down about 1 ½ feet when my shovel hit something. It was not a rock or tree root. I kept digging and after much effort the outline of a rotted box appeared. I was as careful as I could be and finally got the top of the box uncovered. This was difficult, as the box was about one and one-half feet below my feet so I was working on my knees and running out of energy.

The box was about three and one-half feet long, two feet wide and I could not tell how deep. What was in it? I was finally able to pry the cover off the box, more like it disintegrated. With the cover off, we could see bundles of what looked like skin. These were long, thin bundles - GUNS!

Now what? It was getting late and I was out of energy. We should look at one at least. I leaned down and lifted one out. It felt like a gun. I looked for a way to get into the skin, which appeared to be skin like I had never seen before. Perhaps it was sealskin. I was able to unwrap the skin and it was a gun, a lever action rifle in pretty good condition. It had been packed in grease of some kind. The grease had dried out, but the gun looked usable. I looked for a name on the receiver. It was a Winchester, .44-40 caliber. There were several wrapped packages, apparently guns.

Now what? These guns were on county forest property so they belonged to the county. Betty and I discussed what should happen and concluded we would wrap the Winchester up, put it with the others, put the remains of the lid back on and then shovel the dirt back in.

So, it appears the three men killed and scalped were in the gun business, or possibly they were fur traders setting up a business to trade for furs in this wild country of Northwest Wisconsin. Maybe they were killed by rival fur traders who felt their territory was being infringed upon. Why were the guns buried? This whole deal looks very strange. I am sure Benjamin really thought it was strange in the 1870s.

Someday, when we sort out this whole bundle of clues, we will notify the county about these guns and let them deal with their property. I am pretty certain that eventually we will have to let the world know about Benjamin also. That is a different problem. There is a dead body involved! It is also on county forest property, so in order to resolve what happens to Benjamin, I see nothing but giant problems waiting for us.

Chapter 14

~~~~~

We finally get home with the two gold watches and sheath knife. We are exhausted and the work around the farm and our home has suffered. We try to clean up the watches. Water and Formula 409 get most of the grime. One watch had a cover over the face and, after much work, we were able to get it opened. There was an inscription on the inside of the cover. It said, 'To CALEB 6-12-1861.' Was this a birthday gift? From whom? How old was Caleb when he got the watch? Was it given to him before he left for the Civil War? What is his last name?

The other watch had no cover over the face and had no engraving on it. This watch was made by a company called Gillett. Caleb's watch had the name of Walton on it.

These might have been trophies as was the knife and sheath of Benjamin's traps working as he intended. Since they were hidden behind the rocks in the wall it seemed like Benjamin wanted them out of sight but near by. On our next trip back to the den, we will return them, as well as the small metal box. Once again that is property of the county, in their forest.

Chapter 15

~~~~~

I looked at the sheets of paper/skin that had been in the larger metal box. There was one sheet that I had not been able to decipher anything on. Something was there but it didn't make any sense to me. I took it out and rigged up the lights, including the ultraviolet. I could see that something was on the sheet, but what? Finally, I thought about holding the sheet at about a 45 degree angle, shine light from the side and sprinkle pepper on the top of the sheet. If there were indentations from writing, maybe the fine particles of pepper would fall in them and be visible. I sprinkled and, low and behold, the information on the sheet showed itself. It was a map. After a sneeze or two, I realized it was a map of Benjamin's 40 acres.

It showed all four corners, with 1320 feet between each one. It showed compass headings from one corner to the next. It showed that a quarter corner monument was 1320 feet to the west of his northwest corner. The map showed the spring and stream flowing into the lake which is about a quarter mile northwest of his northwest stake. There was a square where his den was. The square was 210 feet to the northwest of his southeast stake. I wondered if Benjamin's stakes may still be there. Being charred in a fire, they would last a long time. If it works out, I will take Benjamin's compass and a long tape measure and see if I can locate that southeast corner. Probably have very little chance of finding it.

Chapter 16

~~~~~

So apparently Benjamin was a General in the Northern Army during the Civil War. I do know that a man could hire his own soldiers by paying them himself, at least for a while. Apparently you could bestow the title of General to yourself under certain conditions. I am pretty sure a person attempting this would have had to be a military person and have a lot of money. This would mean recruiting a large group of platoons and perhaps as big as a brigade. They apparently trained and, when ready, asked to be assigned to do battle. I don't know if Benjamin got to be a General this way.

Since Benjamin had been a surveyor, he more than likely did not have the money to buy an Army. Since he fought in the Indian Wars he maybe had achieved the rank of Lieutenant, or Major by the time he was done fighting the Indians. He could have started out as a Lieutenant or Major in the early days of the Civil War. He could have made promotions as casualties were very high, both from the enemy and also poor health, lousy food and poor equipment, mainly clothes and shoes. Many Civil War soldiers died without ever seeing action. Some brigades lost many more soldiers to sickness than battle injuries.

I contacted the City of Hagerstown, Maryland to see if their census records from the 1860s to 1870s showed a family with the name of Lucy, Caleb and other brothers. The lady in records was very nice, but said that census records for that period and others were damaged in a fire. I asked if there was anyone I could contact and she said she really did not know of anyone. She did give me a phone number for the Hagerstown Historical Society.

A lady answering at the Hagerstown Historical Society told me that looking for that family was a very big job and may involve hundreds of hours. Besides, she doubted the Historical Society had complete enough records to find that family. She told me I was welcome to come and look through their records. I declined at this time.

Contact with the City of Blue Ridge Summit, Pennsylvania produced some results. The lady in the records department found Benjamin Mason listed on school records. He attended schools in Blue Ridge Summit on and off from 1820 to 1836. No address was listed. The lady suggested that he may have lived in the country and not in the city. Also, no middle initial was listed with his name.

A Google search for Benjamin Mason turned up seven Benjamin's connected with the Civil War. None, however, had a middle initial of G. Either our information is faulty or the Civil War records are not complete.

The information on the torn Discharge Document for Benjamin leads us to think he was involved in the bloody battle called The Wilderness. It took place in Virginia in May of 1864. It involved about 100,000 union troops and about 60,000 southern troops. Internet information does not mention Benjamin's name as one of the northern generals. I wonder why. It does not say so, but there may have been 30-40 northern generals under General U. S. Grant and General George G. Mead. Besides, Benjamin may have gotten his Generals star, or stars, as he was discharged. At any rate, Benjamin's trail is not easy to trace.

Chapter 17

~~~~~

Duty at home calls. The second crop hay must be cut and put up. There will be many more hours of tractor time. This means a lot of thinking time.

In the back of my mind, the question of 'what to do with Benjamin's body' is beginning to need answering. There seems to be little more that needs exploring back at the den. It has become clear that Benjamin had great fear of the wrath of Lucy's brothers. What that reason is doesn't seem to be easily found. He came to the land promised to him and basically hid out. He apparently felt he could not contact Lucy as this might alert her brothers as to where he was.

Benjamin apparently felt the brothers would find him so he set his traps to protect himself. It appears his traps killed two and possibly three people, one of which was a Caleb. Maybe this was Lucy's brother. Benjamin hid the two gold watches and a sheath knife as possible trophies of those that were killed by the traps or other means. Benjamin attempted to contact Lucy by way of a telegraph in 1878, many years after he had left Blue Ridge Summit. Perhaps he felt most of the threat to him had passed. Lucy sent no response so maybe she was dead, or moved away or just didn't want to tip off Benjamin's location by responding.

Benjamin led a very Spartan life. I mean it must have been dull. He must have been very patient and very wary, not to leave tracks or call attention to himself. He eventually dies, perhaps working on the escape door in the den. Apparently this ex-surveyor is very skilled in survival as he relies on his own abilities to provide food, shelter and keep himself healthy. What am I missing?

How did his Discharge Document get torn? By him, or someone else? Why was it torn? Was that to show disdain for his service in the Civil War? Did Benjamin tear it in frustration or disgust for his role in the war? There seems to be no trail or record to help answer these questions. The main fact remains that Benjamin G. Mason is lying dead in the den that he built sometime in the 1860s. He died sometime after June of 1878. What should be done with his body and his property which is on county forest property?

Betty and I have had long discussions on what to do and how to do it. The easiest thing to do is forget that we ever found Benjamin and the den. That, however, is impossible since we are already heavily involved in this mystery. We cannot remove any property, or Benjamin, or we will be charged with theft. We are NOT thieves. We know that Benjamin needs a proper burial. Ironically, there is a Northern Wisconsin Veterans Cemetery slightly over one mile from where Benjamin lies at this time. This is a beautiful cemetery built to serve veterans from this part of Wisconsin. Should someone try to get Benjamin interred there? Or, should he be taken back to Pennsylvania to be buried. If so, who will do that? Who will cover expenses, no matter where he is buried? Also, should his body be examined to see how he died? Maybe he was killed. Also, what about the two, or possibly three, people that he may have killed? I guess I know the answer to that. No solid evidence and besides it took place over 130 years ago. The same goes for the three apparent fur traders that were killed near Benjamin's den.

What do we do? Maybe a few more hours driving tractor putting up second crop hay will help. Summer is on the wane and that means fall is not far away. That means small game hunting season starts in September, but by November deer hunting starts and since the county forest here is prime deer country, it means there will be numerous hunters in the forest. Benjamin's den is not as well hidden as it was, as I had to cut some brush and small trees in front of the door. I could not stand the thought of someone vandalizing Benjamin's den. We better get the ball rolling.

Chapter 18

~~~~~

The first thing we must do is contact the county. After all, the forest is their property, as are Benjamin and his artifacts. I served four years on the county board and represented the very land in question. What is the best way to assure that Benjamin gets a proper burial, all the artifacts are properly identified and given, or sold, to the proper people or places? There were some gold coins, silver coins and currency which I imagine the county will keep and sell since budgets are always short.

In due time, I will tell them about the buried rifles in the basement of the apparent fur traders building, 400 yards away. Thinking of those guns, the .44-40 was a popular choice of caliber because its shells could be used in a rifle or a handgun. The shell is quite short and .44 means it is fairly wide. Early settlers, cowboys and such, would be able to interchange ammunition in either weapon.

In my four years on the county board, I spent two years as the chairman of the Board of Supervisors. I didn't exactly want it, but the board elected me by an 11 to 10 vote. Oh, Boy! I could imagine the next two years would mean a lot of meetings and some tough, thorny issues to deal with. I was right on all counts. Out of it all, I did learn how to construct an agenda for full board meetings, as well as the executive committee, which I also chaired. These agendas had to be squeaky clean and must pass muster of our Corporation Council, who is the county's lawyer. There are always persons ready to pounce on any agenda not carefully and skillfully presented. I knew my first stop was the Executive Committee meeting.

I contacted the current Board Chairman and requested time at the next meeting of the Executive Committee to discuss a discovery on the county forest land. He wanted a better explanation, but I said in due time you will know, but for now, please put me on your agenda to make a very short presentation. He agreed and a few days before the executive meeting, I received the agenda and I was on it to make a presentation. What is important here is that the County Board Chairman makes up the full county board agenda with the help of the executive committee and department heads.

Betty and I attended the meeting and when my turn came, I said I had made a discovery in the county forest, of which there are 149,000 acres of county forest in our county. I said I had used various instruments to make this discovery. Since I am a former science teacher, this probably sounded like I had discovered copper or some other metal on county property.

I requested that the full county board go into closed session for me to disclose my discovery. I requested the County Forester, the County Sheriff and Corporation Council be present. I assured them that they would not be disappointed. They granted my request. Surprisingly, there was no opposition. The County Board Chairman assured me that my request would be on the agenda for the August full county board meeting. The ball has begun to roll.

Summer is winding down and a definite date in August has been set. This could result in Benjamin being moved out of his den. It would surely mean a lot of people will know where the den is and will want to see it. Perhaps some would damage it. We needed to visit at least once more and take pictures, plus I wanted to tell Benjamin what we were planning to do with him. I also wanted to see if I could figure out what that humming was.

There was one more thing. I wanted to see if I could find the four wooden stakes that marked Benjamin's property. Since they were charred, it may be possible they are still in place. Besides, on the map of his property there was a small dot about halfway from the spring to the southeast stake. Could that mean something? Or was it just a dent in the paper? I will take the metal detector and a shovel, just in case.

Betty and I loaded up and went back to the den. We tried to walk from our farm sometimes as to not call attention to our comings and goings. That day we rode the four wheeler since we are short of time. We also brought all the papers along and will return them to the large metal box.

We walked in from a different direction each time we approached the den. That day we pried the door open and swung it inward.   The flashlight revealed the fireplace and interior. The humming had started as soon as I pushed the door open. This may sound strange, because I don't believe in ghosts at all.   But I felt Benjamin was responsible for the humming.   We went to the other side of the fireplace and there was Benjamin, just like always.

I started speaking to him. I told him, "I want to

borrow your compass to try to find the stakes you put in so many years ago." I got into the box under Benjamin and retrieved the compass.

The compass appeared to work fine. I then told Benjamin that, " We are going to try to get you an official resting place. A place where many brave soldiers are resting and it is only about one mile from here." I told him that, "We have tried to find Lucy, but have had no luck. It appears that you were able to stop Lucy's brothers from harming you. We want to examine your body to see if someone may have hurt you and that may have caused your death."

"We know you were a brave officer for the United States Army during the Civil War. We also are impressed that you made this nice home for yourself and were able to procure food and take good care of yourself. You appear to be a very resourceful person and I bet we would have liked you, if we could have known you. Good-bye for now. We are going to search for your corner stakes."

Both Betty and I thought the humming was not as loud, but we both thought that was probably wishful thinking.

Chapter 19

~~~~~

We took the compass, metal detector, shovel and tape measure. We first measured out 210 feet toward the southeast. This was from the den door. The stake must be very close. I started looking at the 210 foot mark. I scraped the ground with the edge of the shovel and after a few minutes, I hit a small piece of wood sticking out of the ground. This must be it. I dug down beside it and found Benjamin Mason on one side. That was the southeast corner. If we have the time, we might be able to find the other three stakes.

I was curious about that little mark on the paper halfway from the spring to this stake. We measured the distance from the edge of the spring to that stake. It was 160 feet. Half of that would be 80 feet. We measured that distance and marked the spot. I went to get the metal detector and started sweeping. After about one minute, the detector beeped and beeped! I started digging where the metal seemed to be. After a few shovelfuls, my shovel hit a piece of wood. More digging revealed a wooden box about twelve inches long and eight inches wide. It had been charred also, and appeared solid. I dug around the sides and end. Finally, I could pry it loose from its bed. I reached down to pick it up and found I could barely move it. I got a good grip on it and lifted it out of the shallow hole. Man, it was heavy.

I told Betty it must be gold. The top was just sitting on the box, so I lifted it off. Inside were four gold bars! Each was about nine inches long and two inches wide by two inches deep. There were no marks on any of the bars. This certainly was worth a lot of money. I guess at least three-quarters of a million dollars. Later I figured it out and the approximate value would be one million dollars.

We put the cover back on and put the box back in the hole and covered it up. However, it did not look like the surrounding terrain, so we put branches and other debris to cover it. How did Benjamin get these gold bars here? My guess is that they would have weighed about 13 or 14 pounds each or a total of 54 pounds. Benjamin must have had a horse or mule.

We had talked about this before. What happened to the horse? Benjamin had no hay to feed one during the winter. At least, I don't think he had hay. Maybe he found a swamp nearby and cut some swamp hay. There are some swamps southeast of his den that have large amounts of swamp grass. Maybe he took the horse there when winter started and either tethered it there, or just left it hoping it would still be there in the spring.

Finding that gold was a real surprise. How did Benjamin get that amount of gold? Maybe he was wealthy at one time. Perhaps he got the gold at the expense of Lucy's brothers. Maybe it was confederate gold. Maybe he did buy his own army and make himself a general as a result. It would have been easier to understand if the Discharge Document was not torn in half.

Betty and I returned to the den to put the compass back. We both immediately noticed that there was no humming! It is hard to believe that my talk with Benjamin, dead for at least 135 years, would have caused the humming to stop. Maybe there are ghosts after all. Anyway, I told Benjamin goodbye and promised to visit again soon.

Chapter 20

~~~~~~

The August county board agenda arrived in the mail. Sure enough, at the end of the agenda was the announcement that the full board would go into closed session to listen to information on a recent discovery in the county forest.

The third Tuesday in August rolled around and at 6:00 p.m. the meeting started. After two hours, the board had handled the other items on the agenda. The Chairman cleared the board room, except for the County Forester, County Sheriff and Corporation Council, plus Betty and me.

Betty and I were then given the floor. We had taken pictures inside the den. One showed the fireplace, one showed Benjamin and the two guns and one picture showed the opening of the tunnel. We had made a copy of the patent transferring the government land to Benjamin G. Mason and signed by Martin Van Buren, President of the United States. This was dated April 15, 1839. Also, a copy of the torn Discharge Document was enclosed. Before handing out the packet to each board member and the three invited to stay, I told of how I discovered the door, how I got into the den and briefly what I saw. We next handed out the packets to each of the 21 board members and three others, with instructions that they must all be returned at the completion of the closed session.

The Corporation Council had previously told all those present that whatever is discussed in closed session can not be discussed in any way once the session is over. Penalty could be banishment from the board. I reminded all present that they cannot say anything or it could jeopardize the successful completion of what we would like to see happen.

The packets were passed out and opened. There were many astonished faces and unbelievable words were uttered. Unbelievable was heard from many members. Several questions were presented and answered.

Finally, we were ready to continue. I said, "Our request is that Benjamin G. Mason, a Civil War General for the north, be buried in the Northern Wisconsin Veterans Cemetery, located only a little over one mile from where he now lies. He also should be examined by a forensics lab to see if they can determine how he died. All the artifacts in the den should be documented and perhaps removed as soon as possible. The larger metal box contains some gold coins, silver coins and paper currency. The small metal box in the wall contains gold coins, silver coins and currency, plus two gold watches."

"The den and surrounding area needs to be secured, if possible. It is a crime scene, because apparently either two men, or possibly three, have been killed by a booby trapped shotgun that you see in a picture. There is a deep hole that is now under a fallen tree. There is a skull impaled on a bayonet in the hole. The two gold watches apparently belonged to the men killed. There was also a sheath knife hidden in the wall along with the watches. I take these as trophies taken from victims of Benjamin's traps. These men apparently had some grudge against Benjamin. They are probably Lucy's brothers."

I continued, "I would ask the county to seek permission to bury Benjamin in the Northern Wisconsin Veterans Cemetery. They should ask the Wisconsin Veterans Administration to talk to their counterparts in Pennsylvania to decide where Benjamin should be buried and who should pay for it."

"If Benjamin is to be buried here, I would like to

help plan the ceremony. Betty and I feel a strong attraction to this old man that has been dead for about 135 years."

"I would also ask the County Board Chairman to appoint an ad hoc committee to deal with all aspects of the discovery of Benjamin's den. I would recommend the committee be made up of the County Forest Administrator, the Sheriff, the County Board Chairman, Betty and myself."

Also I said, "Betty and I have not taken anything from the den, or surrounding area. We did take papers home to try to decipher them. We took the watches home to clean them up. All papers and watches have been returned. We admit to doing some digging based on what was in Benjamin's papers. If the county will not charge us for trespassing, we will tell you where to dig and what we found. You will be pleased at what we found."

Several questions were asked by the board members. We answered them as truthfully as we could without giving information about where Benjamin's den was exactly. By now, most have figured out it must be south of our farm, but that means at least 3500 to 4000 acres. Finally, we were winding down, so I asked Corporation Council, "Does it look like we could move

Benjamin and his belongings without getting into legal trouble?" He said, "It is county property so the answer is no, we should not get into any legal problems."

The last thing I wanted the full board to do was agree to make a motion that authorizes the removal of Benjamin and proper disposal of his artifacts. A board member would have to make a motion and be seconded by another board member once the board went back into open session.

I suggested that the motion could say *'I authorize the ad hoc committee to remove the body of Benjamin G. Mason for proper burial, remove his possessions and properly dispose of them and to not press trespassing charges or any other charges for gathering the information presented here.'*

The ad hoc committee will be responsible for any news dissemination. All packets, containing pictures, patents and discharge documents were collected.

In open session, the motion was made and seconded and it passed unanimously. Now the clock was ticking. Even though board members are sworn to secrecy, the word still spreads quickly.

Chapter 21

~~~~~

I asked the Forest Administrator, the Sheriff, and County Board Chairman to meet with Betty and me right after the full board adjourned. We met and tried to set a time when we could go and get this job done. We agreed that the first thing tomorrow is when we should do it. We could drive to within about three-quarters of a mile of the den. We would need a four wheeler and a small trailer to put Benjamin and his possessions on. The Sheriff had such a rig and he offered to bring it. We did not want any sheriff vehicle near the road or, to be seen going in on a forest trail. It was agreed that the County Forester would pick up the Sheriff and the four wheeler and meet at the entrance to the trail at 9:00 a.m. the next day. The Board Chairman would come to our place and ride with us in our pickup, as both pickups would be driven as close to the den as possible. The gate over the trail would be locked after we passed through. We discussed where we are going to put Benjamin. Also, where will we put his belongings, and the coins and currency needs to be in a safe place.

We decided that Benjamin should go to a mortuary so one was contacted in town. It was late and we said we didn't know when, for sure, but we were hoping for tomorrow. That was OK.

We secured a stretcher from the sheriff's department. I hope we have not forgotten anything.

The next day, Betty and I were up early. We packed some sandwiches and soda, loaded the metal detector, several flashlights, a chainsaw and shovel in the truck. We took several large heavy duty garbage bags also.

One problem that I have been wrestling with since I found it - how do we deal with the loaded and cocked 10 gauge shotgun? It is very doubtful that it would ever be cleaned good enough to salvage it. There are apparently two live 10 gauge shotgun shells in the gun. Possibly they won't fire, but maybe they will. I know I would not try to take it apart. How will we get the gun to a safe place. We can't lay it down in a vehicle as it may go off. The only way I could see to transport the gun safely is to have it be standing up in the back of a pick up. I thought on that and came up with a plan.

I rigged a piece of angle iron with pegs that fit the stake pockets of my pickup. I then welded another angle iron in the center of the horizontal angle iron. My plan was to stand the shotgun up next to the upright angle iron that was located in the stake pockets up near the cab of the pickup. I would use bungee cords and fasten the gun to the angle iron.

We all met by the gate which the Forest Administrator had opened. We drove both pickups through and closed and locked the gate. We drove back to a point as close as we could get to the den, which was about three-quarters of a mile from the highway. We unloaded the four wheeler, hooked up the trailer and Betty and I led the way.

We finally arrived at the den. The other three people were amazed at how it blended into the bank. We pried up the door and swung it in. No humming was heard. We had not mentioned this to anyone else. We are not really sure why we did not.

We all crowded into the den. The rest were amazed at what they saw, even though they had seen pictures the night before. While they were looking, I removed the rocks in the wall and removed the small metal box and the sheath knife.

Finally, we brought the stretcher in and positioned it by Benjamin. The Sheriff and Board Chairman gently lifted Benjamin on to the stretcher. He did not fall apart and his clothes and blanket seemed to hold together also. The stretcher was taken outside and put out of the way for now. It was agreed that Benjamin would be the last thing to be loaded. We were very concerned that someone might try to interfere.

We took the large metal box and surveyor chain out and put them next to Benjamin. We used one of the large bags to put the plates, cups, pans, silverware, sharp knives and other utensils, such as the leather cutting scissors. The clothes and shoes were put in another bag.

Next, I crawled into the tunnel and handed out the shovel, saw, adze, axe, brace & bit, traps, hammer, and other small tools. These were put outside also. I brought the metal detector in and asked the Sheriff to sweep the entire interior of the den. It is possible that I may have missed something. When the Sheriff was finished, I asked the Forest Administrator to crawl in the tunnel and sweep it, just in case I missed something. He finished and was happy to get out of the tunnel. It looks like we got Benjamin and all of his possessions outside. Hold it, we forgot the two guns. I took the rifle down and the Board Chairman checked to see if it was loaded. It was, so he unloaded it and put the shells in his pocket. I took the shotgun down and explained that the hammers would not work and the gun would not open after laying outside for maybe 135 years or so. I carried the shotgun outside and carefully laid it on the ground.

I then showed them where the hole was under the downed tree top. The Sheriff and Forest Administrator both crawled in under the tree top and peered down the hole with the use of a flashlight. Sure enough, there was a skull with a bayonet sticking through the top of the skull. It was too far down to reach so it was agreed that it could remain for now. Maybe at a later date we could come back with a chainsaw and shovels and retrieve the skull, bayonet and any other artifacts.

We showed them the spring with the glass jar in it. Apparently Benjamin used this to keep food, mainly meat, cool. We fished out the jar and added that to the load to be forwarded out. We next went up the hill toward the southeast stake of Benjamin's property. We showed him the stake with Benjamin's name on it. They were amazed.

Then we walked back toward the spring, and when I had gone about halfway, I started digging. Since I could see where I had dug before, it did not take long to find the wooden box. After I uncovered it, I asked the Sheriff to lift it out. He tried, but could not lift it out. We dug so he could get his hands under it, and after taking a more balanced stance was able to lift the box and get it out of the hole.

"Man, that is heavy." I asked, "What do you think is in it?" "Gold," was his answer. I pried the cover off and revealed the four gold bars. The three of them looked on in amazement. "It was Gold"! They each picked up a thirteen pound bar and looked at it. "Must be worth a quarter million or more," said the Board Chairman. I said, "More like three quarters of a million."

We filled the hole and each took a bar and Betty carried the box. We carried it down to the den. The thought crossed my mind, could there be more metal in that hole. I took the metal detector and the Sheriff and I went back to the hole and started sweeping. There were no beeps.

We started loading the trailer. Maybe it would all fit. We put Benjamin on the stretcher first. We added the bag of utensils, the tools and there was room for the box with the gold bars. We would carry the guns, metal detector, shovel & flashlights. By this time it was early afternoon. Betty broke out the sandwiches and soda. We all took a break.

As we ate lunch, we discussed how impressed we were by what Benjamin had built and how he had lived. I pointed out where I had found the booby trapped shotgun. I also told the group about how Benjamin had seen several Indians come to the lake to shoot geese and catch fish. Also how the men camped and built a building out of logs over a basement. Apparently they were fur traders, but one night Benjamin heard shots and later saw the cabin was in flames. Days later he investigated and found three dead men. All had been scalped.

We will go quite close to that hole in the ground and we'll show you. Betty and I were curious if there may be anything metal in the hole. We used the metal detector and found several beeps around the edge. We went down in the hole which was about twenty four feet long and not that wide. We started sweeping with the detector and found a place where there were lots of beeps. We started digging and if we have time today we can show you what we dug up.

We slowly started back to the trucks. We followed the same trail out. We had used the chainsaw to cut several downed trees to make a smooth pathway for the four wheeler and trailer. As we got near the hole, I asked if they wanted to take time to dig up what was there. It was the middle of the afternoon by now. They all agreed - let's go find out.

We found the hole and they were amazed again. I started digging and it wasn't long and I was down to the remnants of the top of the wooden box. We cleared the dirt away and took off the remains of the cover. There lay the neat bundles, laying just as we had left them. I reached down and lifted out the same one Betty and I had looked at. The committee unwrapped the skin and were amazed at the condition of the very old rifle inside. ".44-40 caliber," the Sheriff said. "Aren't many of these babies left."

I dug out another bundle and handed it up. "Let's get them out. We can examine them later," said the Sheriff. I kept lifting them out, fourteen in all. "These must be worth a small fortune," said the Board Chairman. "I don't know, but let's have one person remain here to watch over this and fill the hole. The rest take Benjamin and other things and load them on the trucks. Send the four wheeler back for these guns, while two or three stay with Benjamin." The County Board Chairman volunteered to stay with the guns. The rest of us continued to the trucks, which were about a half mile away. It was slow going, but we made it. We unloaded the trailer and the Sheriff took the four wheeler and trailer back for the fourteen guns.

The rest of us started loading the pickups. We needed to save room for the guns on one truck. Benjamin went in first. The stretcher was too long to close the tailgate. A bit of wire from under the seat of my truck secured the stretcher from sliding out. We had a blanket in our truck, so we put that over Benjamin and tucked it under the stretcher. He looked secure. We took the 10 gauge shotgun and, using bungee cords, fastened it to the upright angle iron. That looked strange, but safe and secure. We had no gun case for the Winchester. We put that in the truck the sheriff will be riding in. Let's hope he doesn't fine us for no gun case.

The gold bars and the metal boxes were put in the backseat of the Foresters truck. They would be put in the County Treasurers safe and locked up, hopefully yet that day. We may have to call the treasurer to come back in and open the safe to put the valuables in and lock them up.

It wasn't long before the Sheriff and Board Chairman returned with the guns and shovel. Upon the return of the Sheriff and Chairman, they asked, "what about ammunition for these guns?" Good question, unless who ever killed the traders took it, it must still be in or around the hole. We don't have time to look for the ammunition now, but someone should come back and look at a different time.

The guns were loaded on the Foresters truck to be put in the Treasurers safe, if there was room. The utensils, tools and the two guns from the den could be put in a room in the basement of the jail. On the return trip from the courthouse, Benjamin could be taken to the mortuary.

All the plans were made, so the trailer and four wheeler were loaded up and hooked up to the truck. We turned the trucks around and we headed for the highway. So far everything has gone well. We unlock the gate, drive through and then lock up again. When we reached the trail head, we saw four vehicles parked there. Maybe they were left by people looking for the den.

The County Treasurer was called and she said that she would meet us at the Courthouse. We pulled up by the back door of the Courthouse - Law Enforcement center. The Sheriff unlocked the doors that let us in to the room where we would store the utensils, tools and guns. The Sheriff did not seem concerned about the loaded, rusty 10 gauge double barreled shotgun. About the time we finished unloading those items, the Treasurer arrived and opened her office and the safe. We carried in the gold bars and put them in the charred box. She was impressed!! Next came the metal boxes. We asked her to inventory what we brought in, so she started.

Four gold bars, $1,721 in various paper currency, which was very old, 47 gold coins, 21 silver coins, and two metal boxes. Also one compass, two gold watches, one knife, partial box of .44 caliber shells, partial box 10 gauge shells, two letters and 13 sheets of paper, or skin. There were also receipts for goods purchased. Also the patent and discharge document were included.

And then we brought in one of the guns and asked if she had room for fourteen like it. She said, "Oh, my! It will be tight, but bring them in." She added 14 guns wrapped in skin to her inventory. She put a date and time on the inventory, we all signed it and she made copies for each of us.

We asked the Sheriff to inventory what was in his room. He did: one shovel, one cross cut saw, one adze, one axe, one brace and bit, one surveyors chain, one hammer, 17 assorted traps, assorted small tools, two plates, one cup, two forks, one knife, two sharp knives, two spoons, one frying pan, one kettle, one .44 caliber Winchester, Model 1864, one double barreled 10 gauge (rusted) shotgun, two pair of boots, some clothing, and leather cutting scissors and one jar from the spring. The Sheriff signed and dated it. We all signed and each received a copy of this inventory.

We finally got things put away so we took Benjamin and headed to the mortuary in the next town.

Chapter 22

~~~~~

We called the mortuary and told them we would be there in a few minutes. We arrived and were greeted. The attendant came out as we uncovered the stretcher. He took a look at Benjamin and was aghast! I said, "Meet Benjamin G. Mason, of the Town of Beaver Brook. He passed away about 135 years ago - we think."

After the initial shock, the attendant told us to bring him in. The body was very light weight. We put Benjamin on the examining table. In the bright light Benjamin looked different. We could see he had a gold filling in one tooth. He was completely dehydrated. We could not see any visible signs of trauma. He appeared to be about 5 ft. 6 inches tall and of a slight build, and, maybe weighed 130 pounds. His hair was light colored. He wore no rings or bracelets. There were no tattoo's. He seemed to have all his teeth. He was literally skin and bones. He had a full beard.

Our committee agreed to meet again in two days at 9:00 a.m. We would have had time to think things through from what we had accomplished that day. We need to hold some sort of press conference to tell the people about Benjamin. We need to contact the Northern Wisconsin Veteran's Cemetery to see if Benjamin could be buried there. We need to think long and hard if we need to have his body examined by a forensic lab. The sheriff contacted the county coroner and asked that an official death notice be produced.

What about the wrapped up guns? What will we do with the gold bars, gold coins, silver coins and the currency. I presume that we will sell them and the proceeds go into the general fund for the county. Or should they go to the forestry department? After all, Benjamin, and his belongings, were found on county forest property. We have two days to ruminate on these problems, but I have a feeling it is not going to be easy.

Chapter 23

~~~~~

We had closed the door to Benjamin's Den. Hopefully in time the area will not look so used. We did, however, make a trail right up to about one hundred feet away from it. Someone coming across that could follow it to the den. Oh, well, we can't be there all the time. It does beg the question, what will we do with the den? Should others be told of it so they can marvel at it as we have? Should it be destroyed before someone gets hurt? The county certainly has liability there. We must invite Corporation Council to our meeting in two days. We don't want to get on any slippery slope of legal issues if we can avoid them. Looking ahead it appears that there are lots of hurdles to cross. We do have a good committee and hopefully we can continue to work together and solve all the issues as they are addressed.

I got a phone call the next day. The guy wanted to know if what he heard was true, "that a dead guy was found back in the woods. Was it true?" I can not lie. I said, "Yes, that is true." "Who was it?" "Benjamin G. Mason." "How old was he when he died?" "Maybe 50 or 60 years old." "How did he die?" "We don't know." "OK, thanks," and he hung up. At least he didn't ask some questions that I could refrain from answering. I have a feeling this is the first of a lot of inquiries. Maybe we should have set the meeting up one day. Maybe we should schedule a press news conference for 11:00 a.m. on the day of our meeting.

I checked with the others on the committee and they agreed. Now Betty will email the wire services, newspapers, TV and radio informing them of an upcoming press conference in the county board room of the Courthouse in Shell Lake, Wisconsin at 11:00 a.m. on Friday, August 20th. She briefly stated that the remains of a Civil War Union General have been found in an underground home on county forest property.

The email went on to say that this man had received 40 acres as a reward for fighting for Captain Billy in the Indian Wars. The property transfer, called a patent, was signed by President Martin Van Buren, April 15, 1839. Benjamin didn't come to that property until about 1866. He apparently died sometime after June of 1878. His body was found recently in his underground house. More details will be available at the briefing.

Other thoughts show up on my computer screen.

What if someone shows up and claims to be a relative of Benjamin G. Mason. Is that person entitled to Benjamin's estate? What if a whole bunch of relatives show up? How do we determine if they are bonafide relatives? How do you split the estate up? Better quit thinking about things like that. Sure hope Corporation Council knows the answers to questions like that. This could get wild.

For now, Betty & I need to concentrate on the 9:00 a.m. meeting on Friday. We work on a list of issues that need to be resolved. Who will contact the Wisconsin Veteran's Administration about getting Benjamin G. Mason buried in the Northern Wisconsin Veteran's Cemetery? Also, do we ask if Pennsylvania wants Benjamin back? What if we bury him and then Pennsylvania declares he is one of their soldiers and want us to send him back? That could take an act of the legislature of both states.

What about the Gold Bars? Would they be considered part of Benjamin's estate? They really were not close by, but they were found on what was his property at one time. Lawyers could have a great time with this, especially when at least three-quarters of a million dollars is involved. For certain, the 14 wrapped up guns are not part of Benjamin's estate. We could develop a plan to sell them and not be looking over our shoulder. I bet the County Treasurer wants them out of the safe. I can't blame her, they take up quite a bit of room, and besides they are somewhat gross looking.

The gold coins must be worth many thousands of dollars. The paper currency may be valuable for collectors, as are the silver coins. Perhaps we need to make a legal notice in our local newspaper, establish a waiting period and then if no one shows up we can decide on a plan to sell any or all of Benjamin's estate. I really think we should do something about that rusty, loaded and cocked 10 gauge double barreled shotgun. I am going to try to get the committee to do something about it very soon as it could be very dangerous. It also could be very valuable if it could be cleaned up. One of our committee thought it was an L. C. Parker. That is a quality name in shotguns. Perhaps we should advertise on eBay and try to get it out of the counties control and liability.

Chapter 24

~~~~~

It is late summer around the farm. It has been another dry summer, the sixth in a row, so hay and pasture yields are reduced. In the next two weeks or so we will put up corn silage. We had a big wind recently and with over five miles of fence, I need to check the fences, especially near trees to detect a downed fence. I don't want a repeat of what got me into this giant problem, which means cows could get out if a fallen tree knocks down the fence. Life goes on around the farm, so I will do the best to work around Benjamin. I did see a fisher, which is a mean weasel family member, a covey of partridge and a pileated woodpecker as I checked the fence. It is a nice job, if I am not rushed for time and the mosquitoes and deer flies are not hungry.

The 9:00 a.m. meeting on Friday begins. Corporation Council is present. I sure hope he has answers that we want to hear. We shall see. The County Board Chairman runs the meeting with the usual efficiency for a county committee meeting. We have no printed agenda, but the Chairman has obviously been doing some heavy duty thinking also. We get right to the point. He found out that the mortuary will keep Benjamin for as long as needed. No price was mentioned. The Chairman will contact the Wisconsin Veteran's Administration to see if Benjamin can be put to rest here or will Pennsylvania want him back.

The Chairman also has gotten heat from the County Treasurer. She doesn't mind the boxes and the gold bars, but ------ those guns wrapped in skins have got to go. What should we do? The Sheriff thinks we should try to sell them on eBay. From what I know about it, it seems good to me. Corporation Council says alright. We vote to do that. We also know that idea would need to be approved by the County Board, or perhaps the County Forestry Committee.

The Chairman brought up the gold coins, currency and silver coins. Corporation Council jumps in and tells us we must publish the news of Benjamin G. Mason's death as a legal notice in our local newspapers. He also tells us that since we know he was from Blue Ridge Summit, Pennsylvania, we should place legal notices in that city's newspaper also. We asked about the gold bars and Corporation Council said they would be considered part of Benjamin's estate as are the utensils, tools, watches, guns, boots and clothes. If someone comes forward, we will have to study their claims and go from there. Apparently Benjamin did not leave a will. How about the den? What do we do with it? Corporate Council says the county has liability as it is. Perhaps the county should put a chain link fence around it for the time being. The County Forestry Committee has the responsibility to deal with issues that could be a liability. Corporate Council recommends the Forestry Administrator put it on the next meeting agenda and quickly deal with it. He may want to call a special meeting of the Forestry Committee and quickly reduce the risk of liability. The Forester agreed and said he will act quickly. For the time being, the hole in the ground, with the skull skewered on a bayonet, is not a problem being that it is under a huge tree top.

The next issue is the upcoming press news conference. Our committee agreed that the County Board Chairman should run the conference with the rest of the committee, plus Corporate Council there to help out, if needed.

We spent the next few minutes preparing for the conference. We finished stating what we wanted to tell and the Chairman asked his assistant to type it and produce several copies. With these in hand, we headed to the conference. We also had the same packets given out to the full board on Tuesday. These contain three pictures and two documents.

Chapter 25

~~~~~

We got to the board room early and it was already nearly full. Several television stations were there and many reporters, plus a lot of people with microphones, apparently for radio. This looks like it could turn out bad. The packets are passed out and the Chairman begins the conference. With such a large turnout, extra packets were made and passed out. He tells everything that was in the notice of the press conference. He asked for questions and it was an instant show of shouting and waving. Finally, the Chairman got people calmed down and pointed to individuals to ask questions. Most questions were routine about the den, Benjamin G. Mason and why he got his land. Finally, one reporter asked what was he running from? The Chairman asked me to answer. I told him of the two letters from Lucy and the feeling that there was some kind of feud between Benjamin and Lucy's brothers. The same reporter asked if the brothers ever showed up? The answer is they probably did.

I said, "Benjamin indicated in writings that he had set some traps. He had 10 gauge shotgun shells, but no shotgun in the den. I started looking, using a metal detector and I found a rusted 10 gauge double barrel shotgun, laying on the ground, both triggers cocked and ready to fire. The gun was very rusty and does not work, but it is still loaded. I later found two gold watches behind the rocks in the den. One was engraved with the name CALEB and dated 1861. I think these were watches of two of Lucy's brothers killed by a booby trapped shotgun. No proof of it though." I did not mention the hole with the skull impaled on the bayonet. Glad no one asked.

One representative of a television station wanted to know if he could visit the site. Oh, Boy! We had not thought of that. It was public land so there was no way we could keep anyone away. Our committee huddled and agreed that we should show the site to anyone that wanted to see it. As long as we were with them it should be alright. We told the news people that, yes they could visit. It is at least one and a half miles from the highway. We could take pickups, or vans, to within three quarters of a mile of the den. From there it would be walking over rough terrain in the hardwood forest.

Since it was nearly lunchtime, we told the group that we would meet outside the Law Enforcement building at 1:00 p.m. We warned people that they would need some good walking shoes and there might be mosquitoes and deer flies. Deer ticks and wood ticks are also a possibility.

Then the light came on! We had some of Benjamin's belongings stored in that building. Perhaps we could let the news people in to see the tools, utensils, and two guns.

We went to the room where the artifacts were stored. Could we put them in the meeting room which was much larger? A check on the rooms schedule showed it was open. We got busy and carried the tools and utensils out and put them on tables. We figured that in this particular case, we would bring out the two guns and hold them and not let anyone touch them. What if all these folks want to go to the den? There were about 35 people. There is parking at the trail head off the highway. To walk the entire distance of one and a half miles would not work for many of them. Perhaps we could put them in the back of pickups and carefully drive as far as we could. Our committee had three pickups and at 7-8 people per truck we would be short if they all wanted to go. Hopefully one or two news people would have a pickup, or van, to haul some people.

The folks returned from lunch and nearly everyone came back. We explained that most of the artifacts were on display on tables downstairs in the meeting room. They were excited. Down we went and they were impressed by what they saw. How old it was and how little was there. This man must have lived with just the bare minimum. No coffee pot? No razor? No clothes washing equipment? No clock? Many comments.

We brought in the two guns. The shotgun was an ugly mess. It was still loaded so we were very careful how we handled it. We explained that we intended to deal with the shotgun very soon. No decision has been made on what will be done.

We finally went back up to the parking lot. The Sheriff, Betty and I returned everything to its room and locked the door. We had already asked folks to carpool to lessen the burden of vehicles at the trail head. There were 30 news people, and one person had a van that they offered to drive back on the trail. Another had a small pickup and also offered to take some people.

We got our convoy started. I would have to stop to get our flashlights. The Sheriff had flashlights also. At the trail head we loaded up and the five vehicles slowly headed on the trail. It took a few minutes, but we stopped and everyone got out.

The three-quarters of a mile hike to the den took about a half hour. On the walk to the den, many comments about the beautiful forest were heard. I think for many of these people, this was the first time to be so far away from a road and so deep in a large forest. Finally, we arrived there. Many pictures of the door were taken. Next we pried the door up and swung it inward. One by one, they were given a flashlight and allowed in through the small doorway.

I stayed in to answer any questions. There was complete amazement about the construction of the fireplace and roof structure. To think it was built over 140 years ago and still seems strong today. Three people crowded into the tunnel and were happy to come back out.

Eventually, all had a chance to go in the den. Many pictures were taken and television footage was run. All the news services were there, as were at least five television stations. All the local and regional newspapers were present, including Milwaukee and Madison papers.

While waiting to go in the den, the Forester showed people the spring. He also showed them the escape door which was near the spring. This was at the other end of the tunnel. Complete amazement was a commonly heard comment.

By now everyone had the opportunity to go in the den, and we felt that we should tell the group about the hole in the ground with the skull on the bayonet. It was bound to come out some time.

We asked if anyone wanted to crawl into the downed tree top and look down the hole. Nearly everyone wanted to. This surprised us. Anyway, they took turns and peered down the hole and once again were amazed at what they saw. Benjamin must have had good reason to fear Lucy's brothers, or other people. I reminded them of seeing the Indians. I didn't want to explain about the fur traders cabin, the fire and death, and the scalping of the three men.

We began walking back to the vehicles. Someone wanted to know where Benjamin was and if they could they see him. Our committee was not ready for that. We were able to discuss it and thought, why not! The Sheriff called the mortuary and explained about our group wanting to see Benjamin G. Mason. The mortician agreed and said he would have Benjamin available in a few minutes. We passed the word on that we would be able to see Benjamin at the mortuary.

Our group got back to the trucks and van, then back to their vehicles at the trail head. We headed for the mortuary and by this time it was nearly 4:00 p.m. The group filed in to look at Benjamin. Hardly a word was spoken. It appeared that the sight of this dead man, dead for around 135 years, or more, was enough to put this group in awe. Benjamin G. Mason was an impressive sight. Many pictures were taken, television footage was shot and many notes taken.

Finally, it looked like the group had enough for one day. This day was far different than what we had expected. We probably could have planned things better than we did, but it sure turned out great. We certainly got great comments from the group of news people. One lady said it was by far the longest news conference she had ever been at! We were all ready to call it a day. I wonder what happened at the farm today.

Chapter 26

~~~~~

The next morning the Forester called. He said he had researched the State Statutes. He found that basically it said that any artifacts found on property owned by the county, and enrolled as county forest property, belonged to the county that the forest is enrolled in. This includes homesteads, buildings, structures and any artifacts on, or in, the ground. This was good news. The Forester had already consulted with the County's Corporation Council and after he read the statutes, he agreed.

This means that we don't have to publish any legal notices. Heirs could not come forward and claim Benjamin G. Mason's estate. The County Board Chairman called a meeting of our ad hoc committee for Tuesday morning to decide what to do with the property. Also, to see if any progress has been made about getting Benjamin buried.

By Friday evening, several television stations ran news clips of Benjamin. The coverage was enthusiastic and good. The Saturday evening news on two national television networks carried about five minutes on Benjamin. The coverage was excellent. Now the whole country would know about Benjamin G. Mason and his reclusive life in his later years.

Perhaps people in Hagerstown and Blue Ridge Summit may see these programs and be able to answer some of the questions that still need answers.

Duty on the farm calls. This has been another dry summer. We did get a little timely rain on one large field, and there is some third crop alfalfa to cut and round bale. Saturday morning, I hook up the discbine and go cut 35 acres of pretty decent hay. Another 3 ½ hours of tractor time to think of what, and how, things need to get done.

In the middle of this field is a huge white pine tree. Several years ago, a pair of bald eagles carried branches up to near the top of this huge tree and built a large nest about five feet wide and three feet deep. They have raised one eaglet each year until this year, when they raised two. As I ride around cutting the hay, I see these two nearly full grown eaglets standing on the edge of the nest, or on a limb, stretching their wings, getting ready to fly. That is an impressive sight. Just one of the many rewards for living where we do.

Sunday, I get a call from the County Board Chairman. One of the television channels from the Twin Cities wants to interview him. He wants me to be with him to offer support and help out with some questions. They would send a crew and meet us at the court house. Hopefully, we can show them some of the artifacts and keep our fingers crossed that they don't ask questions we don't want to answer, like gold coins, silver coins, currency and gold bars.

Our committee may resolve that on Tuesday. I guess that until we have a plan, and it is approved by the full County Board, it really isn't a plan. Time will tell. We are very willing to tell the world about Benjamin, but we understand that our discovery could open old wounds that occurred in, or around, the Civil War. The persons involved may be long dead, but their deeds may have been so dreadful that grudges may have been carried on for decades. We all realize there is a risk in finding out some long silent revelations.

On Monday morning, the Board Chairman and I meet with the television crew. We start out by showing the artifacts from the den. The rusty double barreled 10 gauge shotgun seems to be of great interest to the interviewer. He seems to focus on the fact that gun was rigged to shoot someone. That seemed wrong to him. I told him of the two letters from Lucy, and that Benjamin felt so strong that he had to protect himself.

I told him about Benjamin stating the traps were set. Since there was only one shotgun, there must have been another trap. I searched with a metal detector and found the hole under the downed tree. In the hole is a human skull with a bayonet stuck in it. I told of finding the watches and sheath knife. Things were very different in the 1860s and '70s. The Civil War was just completed and Benjamin G. Mason was a Union General. Killing and death were an everyday fact of life, so rigging these traps probably came as second nature to Benjamin. The interviewer seemed to realize that Benjamin lived in a very different time, and a very different place, than people live today.

Next came the question of why did Benjamin come to northern Wisconsin. The Board Chairman presented a copy of the patent. The interviewer was amazed. First of all, he didn't know a document like that ever existed. Secondly, he was amazed, "Captain Billy and the Indian Wars!" Then came, "And signed by Martin Van Buren, the President of the United States of

America and dated April 15, 1839 AD."

So Benjamin was presented this 40 acres in 1839, but did not come here until much later. For one thing, Benjamin fought in the Civil War as a Union Soldier. Apparently, something happened during the Civil War involving Lucy's brothers who may have been from Hagerstown, Maryland. Benjamin was from Blue Ridge Summit, Pennsylvania, very close by.

The interview continued. "So Benjamin lived in a den? Is it possible to go there and see it?" My hay was not going to get dry today, so I agreed to take the crew to the den. This was alright with the County Board Chairman and he declined going along. The crew followed me to the forestry office and I got a key for the gate, plus I got permission from the Forester to drive on their property. The crew parked their vehicle at the trail head and rode in the back of my pickup as far as we could go.

We walked the three-quarters of a mile to the den. I had a flashlight with me and I opened the door and swung it inward. I invited the crew into Benjamin G. Mason's den. They were flat out 'very impressed' with the quality of stonework and the eight large timbers making up the roof of the structure. This man lived in this small space, using a fire only at night because he was afraid for his life. He lived mostly on a meat diet and much of it must have been dried. He was a real hermit. Something powerful must have happened to make a Union General live like he appeared to have lived.

The crew wrapped up and we went back to the truck. On the way back, the interviewer asked, "Where is Benjamin now?" I told him and he asked if it was possible to see him. I called the mortuary and if we got there soon, we could visit Benjamin G. Mason.

The crews reaction was similar to the other news people. Very little talking and much footage was shot. Finally the interviewer said, "This is the most amazing story I have ever covered. To look far back into history to a time when this part of Wisconsin was unsettled, except for Indians."

He promised to make a half-hour program to be sold to a national network. The crew wrapped up and headed back to their studio. It was late afternoon, with just enough time for me to get home and rake up the 35 acres of alfalfa to be baled the next afternoon.

Chapter 27

The next morning our ad hoc committee met. The Corporation Council was present also. The Chairman developed an agenda and posted it in the appropriate places. First thing was a report from the Forester on what the Forestry Committee had for a recommendation. This committee got right into Benjamin's den. They realized that many people would want to see the den. They felt the county should try to be as cooperative as possible. They recommended that the entire area around the den be swept with good metal detectors to see if any other booby traps exist. Also, perhaps find the places where Benjamin's victims of the booby traps might be buried. Also, they want to have the head of the county maintenance carefully inspect the den for its structural soundness. The tunnel needs to be sealed off so no one can enter it.

The committee recommended that a plan be developed to allow vehicles to drive back to within ¾ of a mile of the den. The County needs to make a temporary small parking area for up to 20 vehicles. Also, they need to hire personnel to allow vehicles in on the trail at the trail head. Another person, both with radios, to control the number of vehicles, and since the road is so narrow, one way traffic must be assured by use of the radios. The trail from the temporary parking lot back to the den should be improved and well marked.

The trail back to the temporary parking lot is a multi use trail. It is now designated as a mountain bike trail, but it is also a logging road, when needed. People can hike on it, cross country ski, ride snowmobiles and all terrain vehicles. It is managed by the County Forestry Department and winds through some beautiful stands of hardwoods, that are also managed by the Forestry Department.

This program to allow visitors to the den should continue until the end of October. Expenses would be paid out of proceeds from selling some artifacts. The program should be put on a fast track since it was already late August. The County Forestry Committee certainly has been very involved and very positive in their handling of Benjamin. They deserve high marks for their involvement.

That was certainly good direction from the Forestry Committee. The Board Chairman reported that the Wisconsin Veteran's

Administration was very interested in having Benjamin buried at the Northern Wisconsin Veteran's Cemetery. They have approved Benjamin's interment there. They have contacted the Pennsylvania Veteran's Administration and were waiting to hear from them. We asked Corporation Council if artifacts found on county forest land belong to the county as the Forester had found out. He assured us that it was true and he recommended that we develop a plan to dispose of everything found in, and around, the den.

We entered into a discussion of how we would dispose of the artifacts. We thought our best route would be to hire an agent, or agency, to dispose of the coins, currency, gold and gold watches. This should be done over the internet, but also be made available to anyone not on the internet. Advertisements to hire an agent was approved.

Discussion of what to do with the tools and utensils followed. It was recommended that they be given to the County Historical Society. The papers, or skins, also be given along with the metal boxes to the County Historical Society. Any clothing and boots would also go to the County Historical Society.

The two guns and ammunition should be offered on eBay. The 10 gauge double barreled shotgun must be clearly sold as a loaded, rusty, dangerous gun. Corporation Council recommended that the County Board Chairman call an emergency meeting of the full County Board of Supervisors very soon.

The meeting was finished and Betty and I headed for home. I hooked up the big round baler, applied grease where needed, and added twine. I fueled up the tractor and headed for the hay field. More time to think. Things sure seem to be falling into place. There is a lot of great coverage on television, radio and newspapers, including periodicals. This has caused the Court House and Administrative Coordinator to be bombarded with calls, emails and visits. Benjamin was at the center of a lot of attention.

The emergency County Board meeting was held and they approved all that was asked for. The Forestry Department began developing an enlarged parking area and improving the trail back to the den. Two people with high quality metal detectors were hired to sweep the entire area around the den. The County Maintenance Department Head inspected the structural soundness and it was judged as OK. He recommended that people not be allowed on the roof of the den. To that problem, he put stakes with yellow tape outside the outline of the roof to keep people from going on it. He also put a metal grate over the opening to the tunnel and attached a sign warning "NO ENTRY".

Chapter 28

~~~~~

Advertisements for an agent to deal with the coins and gold were placed in appropriate sources. The guns were posted on eBay and immediately received activity. The Winchester carbine was at $1,879. The 10 gauge double barreled shotgun started at $1,244. The County Historical Society came and looked at the tools and utensils. They will get back to us.

The publicity produced numerous responses. Most of them were in awe of the entire story of Benjamin. There were some suggestions about what could have happened to cause the bad blood between Benjamin and Lucy's brothers. One day, a letter came to me from a lady by the name of Susan Ford, postmarked Hagerstown, Maryland. She identified herself as a Civil War buff, especially dealing with Regiments from Maryland. She said that the Union 3rd Regiment Potomac Home Brigade Infantry was organized at Cumberland, Hagerstown and Baltimore, Maryland the end of October 1861 to the end of May 1862. Twenty-four men from Hagerstown were part of this 3rd Regiment. On May 5-7 of 1864, they were engaged in the Battle of the Wilderness. Several of the Hagerstown soldiers took part in that battle. Also in the battle, was the Union 69th Regiment Infantry, Pennsylvania volunteers. These soldiers were also fighting the rebels in the Battle of the Wilderness. One of the officers for the 69th was a General by the name of Mason. Fighting was fierce, but several soldiers from the 3rd Regiment, the Maryland boys, were killed and wounded by friendly fire from the 69th, Pennsylvania boys. Very hard feelings developed between these units, even though they were both a part of the Union Army.

Also in the Battle at the Wilderness, a shipment of rebel gold was captured as it had inadvertently taken the wrong road on its way to Richmond. The rebels claimed there were 35 gold bars on that shipment. Union records showed only 30 gold bars were captured.

Susan's letter continued that the soldiers of the 3rd Regiment claimed the 69th soldiers stole the 5 bars of gold. Apparently the 69th had captured the gold from the southern soldiers. The 3rd Regiment soldiers demanded a share of the missing gold. Apparently it did not happen. A subsequent investigation ruled that there was no missing gold. If this was General Mason from Blue Ridge Summit, Pennsylvania, that might explain the hard feelings. Several boys from

Hagerstown very likely fought for the 3rd Regiment. There is a strong possibility that one, or more, of Lucy's brothers were involved with this dispute that occurred in the Battle of the Wilderness.

If Susan Ford's letter was correct, it confirms what many of us thought could have happened to cause such hatred. Apparently the 3rd Regiment soldiers thought the 69th soldiers stole 5 bars of gold. Since one of their officers was a General Mason, he looked like the candidate for their ire. Another question came up. If the four bars that were found near Benjamin's den were indeed what Susan is suggesting, what happened to the other one? Did Benjamin have them when he came to his land in Wisconsin? If he did, could they be buried someplace near the den?

I got the idea that I better take another look at Benjamin's papers. Betty and I took our ultraviolet light and went to the County Treasurers office, as that is where the large metal box is kept. We retrieved the box and went to the sheriffs office with the papers.

We also gave the Sheriff a copy of Susan Ford's letter. We set up our light and arranged the papers. We looked and we could not see anything that looked like a mark on the papers. We seemed to be at a dead end, when Betty said, "What about by one of the stakes marking the property?" We looked at the map again. There does seem to be an irregularity by the south east stake. It does appear to be an indentation very close to the notation for the stake. The other stakes did not have indentations. Maybe something might be buried there. As soon as possible, I will take a shovel and metal detector and see what I can find.

I roll out of bed at 4:30 a.m. next morning. That's Oh Dark Thirty by my standards. I head back to the den on my four wheeler. By now I can drive right up to the den. I take the metal detector and shovel and head to the south east stake location. I started sweeping near the stake and 'bingo'! The detector beeped. Something metal is down there. I start digging and, about a foot down, my shovel hits something. I dig some more and find a gold bar. Not in a box, but just in the ground. I lift it out. It is about the same size as the other gold bars found earlier. The metal detector did not beep again near the hole, or in the hole. I wondered if there was a gold bar buried by the other three stakes? We have recovered five gold bars. Apparently five bars were missing at the Wilderness Battle in 1864. If those bars were

Standard Industrial Gold Bars they would have weighed about 27 ½ pounds each. The bars we have found only weigh about half that weight, or 13 ½ pounds. There are no markings on our bars, and they are about half the weight of the missing confederate gold. Did Benjamin have an accomplice so he split the booty with that person?

Did they melt the original gold bars and recast them into smaller bars? A foundry could probably do that. Was Benjamin's accomplice able to access a foundry?

I favor the idea that Benjamin has only five gold bars. If others are buried here, perhaps the people hired to sweep the area will find them. Being worth about a quarter of a million dollars each, it may be tempting to not mention that they found any gold bars. I prefer to think that these people would report the bars, if they found them.

I took a good look at the gold bar. I cleaned off the dirt and looked for a mark of any kind. There was no mark that I could see. I was pretty sure that gold bars have some markings on them. I think the assayers mark for purity is on a bar. Perhaps the gold was melted down and recast into a different shaped bar. If the gold was stolen it would be a good idea to get rid of any identifying marks. This discovery and Susan Ford's letter seem to make Benjamin look like a criminal.

Chapter 29

~~~~~

Because I have the metal detector and the shovel, I decide to look for any ammunition at the fur trader site. Today the basement hole has sloping sides, probably caused by agents of erosion, like freezing and thawing. I try to determine where the edge of the original hole was. I began sweeping that line on the west side of the hole. Halfway down the wall, I get a beep.

I start digging on the sloping surface, which makes digging difficult. About two feet down, I strike a metal box. The box is very rusty and it takes several minutes to free the box from its bed in the dirt. Finally, I am able to get a hold on the box and lift it out. It is very heavy and about 18 inches by 12 inches by 8 inches deep.

Since the box is so heavy, I struggle to put it down where I can examine it and see if I can open it. It requires some prying with the shovel, but the cover is finally off. The box is full of smaller boxes of ammunition! Bullets are made out of lead and lead is very dense, not as dense as gold, but close.

There are many boxes of .44-40, .38-40, .38-55

and .25-20. The box had done a good job of protecting the boxes of shells. Only a few showed any sign of deterioration.

I calculated that the box had been placed in a hole in the wall of the basement, and not in the floor as the guns were. Perhaps some piece of furniture was in front of the box location and who ever killed the traders was not able to find it. That heavy box and the gold bar were difficult to load onto the four wheeler, but I got them secured and headed home.

I took the gold bar to the treasurers office and put it with the other four bars. The box with the ammunition was put with the guns in the Law Enforcement Building. I called the other committee people and told about finding one more gold bar, plus the ammunition, from the fur traders basement. I had already given a copy of Susan Ford's letter to each of the committee members, so now they could get their wheels turning, too. I wonder who Susan Ford is? Is she a legitimate Civil War buff, or is she a trouble maker. She listed a phone number so I thought I should try to call her.

I wanted someone else to be on the phone with me besides Betty. I asked the Sheriff and he agreed as long as it could be that day, as he had to go out of town. We went to his office so we could use the speaker phone. I called Susan Ford and she answered. We exchange pleasantries and then I asked her about her research. She explained that, "her great, great, great, great grandfather Ford fought in the Civil War. And since he lived at Hagerstown, he joined up when the 3rd Regiment Potomac Home Brigade Infantry was organized at Hagerstown from late October 1861 to the end of May 1862. Local historians had done a good job of recording the service of this Regiment. They fought at Franklin, Harpers Ferry, defended Baltimore, Fredrick City and other places and battles. They were mustered out on May 29, 1865. My great, great, great grandfather Ford was in the Army fighting Indians in the 1880s. My great, great grandfather Ford was with Teddy Roosevelt during the Spanish-American War. My great Grandfather Ford fought in World War I and my Grandfather Ford fought in World War II. My father fought in Vietnam. I am a spinster and an only child so the fighting Fords line ended with my Dad."

Susan continued, "With a pedigree like that, I felt compelled to find out as much as I could about each of these men, who they were, where they fought and what they did with their lives. This is why I responded to the television news story from Wisconsin. I already knew considerable because it involved men that my great, great, great, great grandfather fought with before some were transferred to the 3rd Regiment."

We were impressed with Susan Ford's knowledge because she sure seemed to be able to espouse information at the drop of a hat. We had called her cold. We asked if she possibly knew anything about a lady by the name of Lucy from Hagerstown, that also had a brother by the name of Caleb. He apparently fought in the Civil War and may have joined the 3rd Regiment with your great, great, great, great grandfather. She said she didn't know Lucy. She would try to find a list of all the Hagerstown soldiers that joined in 1861 and early 1862. If she found a Caleb she would let us know. I told Susan Ford I was surprised that the Potomac Home Brigade Infantry, Regiment Infantry and the Eastern Shore Regiment were all Union troops, but were all from Maryland, even though Maryland is south of the Mason-Dixon Line. Susan responded that, "Yes, Maryland was a southern state, but most of the state had very little interest in the slavery issue which was the main issue of the Civil War. Maryland remained a Union State, but there were several locations such as Harpers Ferry that were on the Confederate side. A Captain Bradley T. Jackson, later Brigadier General, organized a troop of about 500 Maryland soldiers and they were mustered into the service of the Confederate State in May of 1861. There was considerable sentiment to support the secessionist, but the overwhelming support was for the Union in its struggle with the confederacy."

We asked Susan what her profession was and she replied that, "I own and operate an abstract company in Hagerstown."

We thanked Susan for taking the time to talk to us. The Sheriff and I were satisfied that Susan Ford was indeed a very credible source of information and her letter should be considered bonafide.

I was reminded of a visit Betty and I made several years ago as we passed through north central Alabama. We visited a Natural Bridge attraction which was privately owned. We visited the impressive Natural Bridge and on the way out, we came to the owner, sitting near the entrance. He inquired of how we liked the bridge. We responded very positively, then he wanted to know where we were from. We told him,

Wisconsin. He said he already knew that from our accent and besides, "I saw the license plate on your car."

This older man was an interesting visitor. He asked, "Do you realize that troops from Alabama fought for the Union in the Civil War?" Of course we did not know that, because if there was a southern state, Alabama would be on the top of the list. This was after all the happenings at Selma, Birmingham and other places involving voter registration.

The older gentleman asked if we had ever heard of the Hatfield's and the McCoy's. Of course we had, and he said that took place near here and it was over one clan supporting the south and one clan supporting the Union. He said, "If you get a chance to visit our county courthouse, you will see a statue of a Civil War Soldier with a Confederate flag over one shoulder and the Stars & Stripes over the other shoulder." We visited with this gentleman, thanked him for his information and continued on our way. In a few miles, we came to a town and the road took us past a square with the courthouse on it. There was the statue of the Civil War Soldier with the two flags over his shoulder! We were very impressed. How that must have torn people apart. This was quite an eye opening experience. Growing up in the 20th century, near a small northern town, my view of what happened to start the Civil War was definitely very much one sided. Also, I am reminded of some of the very tough choices people had to make in their life. Today, political choices can cause family feuds as can many other issues. I guess man is destined to have disagreements. That is sad, but true.

Chapter 30

~~~~~

Now the road takes another turn. It appears that Benjamin G. Mason could not resist temptation and perhaps took the gold with the help of an accomplice. He apparently melted the gold and recast it to remove any foundry marks, or assayers quality marks. It appears, for now, that Benjamin ended up with half of the gold bars. I wonder who his accomplice was? Another General? A civilian from Virginia near the Wilderness?

Once again my computer is running wild. What really happened? It was so long ago that we will probably not ever know the truth. What if the gold currently stored in the treasurers safe was stolen from the Confederates at The Wilderness? If the county felt it should be returned, who would they return it to? The Confederacy certainly is not a sovereign nation even though it apparently was their gold in 1864. Maybe they stole it. From whom? Gold and currency was needed to pay troops, buy supplies and medicine, buy horses and mules, buy weapons and gunpowder, along with many, many other things, to keep an army of hundreds of thousands in fighting shape. People were desperate to win battles.

These are questions we will only be able to guess at what the answers are. We can see a fuzzy picture on the computer of things happening so long ago, that they are nearly impossible to bring into focus. Benjamin left the turmoil of the Civil War and very hard feelings to come to Wisconsin and deliver a giant headache on our doorstep. Never mind that over 130 years have passed and nearly seven generations of time and change have occurred. The problem is on our windshield now.

It appears that Benjamin was a thief!! Even though he appears to be a General in the Union Army, he somehow could not resist temptation and with help, stole the gold bars now resting in the safe at the County Treasurers office. This is beginning to tax my brain.

Chapter 31

~~~~~

Meanwhile, the corn is in the dent stage. That means that when you take an ear of corn and peel back the husk, the individual kernels will have a little dent in each one. A few days before that, the corn would be in the dough stage and before that in the milk stage. It is now in the dent stage so I have made arrangements with my good friend and neighbor to chop the corn into silage and put it into a long narrow pile, pack it very well to get air out and cover it with plastic to keep rain out.

John, his father and uncle will come with a large John Deere tractor to power the two row chopper. They will bring three Badger self-unloading wagons and another large tractor. I will provide another large John Deere and a John Deere loader tractor to push the silage up on the pile and pack it. There are only 16 acres to chop and we hope to get 40 loads and perhaps get it all done in one day.

It has been a dry summer, so we will probably only get 30 loads or so. Time will tell. With all those tractors running, wagons carrying silage and unloading, experience tells us that things can go wrong. John and his father are excellent farmers and plan ahead for what might go wrong. They have some spare parts, extra tires and wheel bearings with them, along with a pocket full of luck. We will have a nice pile of high quality corn silage when we are finished.

I will start feeding silage to the cows and calves about the middle of September. The cows love the stuff and when I call them, they will come in from the summer pastures. The calves will follow their mothers so by the middle of October we will let them all in, close the gates and separate the cows from the calves. This is the process of weaning and neither party likes it, so there is a lot of mooing and bawling. We will put the calves into our tub corral and then into the squeeze chute to give them all their shots, wormer, new age and source ear tags and neuter the bull calves.

This is a big day on our farm, and I have found out that much preparation goes into being sure the corrals are secure and all the gates are as they should be. We can always use some luck. Once in awhile, a calf slips through, so we must sort it out and run it through again.

These are really nice calves from Black Angus Registered bulls and mostly black cows. We will feed the corn silage and our best second and third crop alfalfa hay to them. They will be loaded into a large semi truck in early January and sent to a large feeder sale in Minnesota. These calves are age and source verified so they are eligible to be sold to an overseas buyer.

Chapter 32

~~~~~

The County Board Chairman has called a special meeting to deal with the plan put forth by the Forestry Committee allowing people to visit Benjamin's den. We also need direction on what to do with the gold bars. Our ad hoc committee planned to meet one hour before the full board meeting. The Corporate Council was invited to the first meeting.

In our ad hoc committee meeting, we got right to the issue of the gold bars. The Sheriff, Betty and I reported on our conversation with Susan Ford in Hagerstown, Maryland. From what Susan's letter said, it appears that Benjamin may have stolen the gold bars from the Confederate soldiers in the Battle of the Wilderness. Benjamin may have had an accomplice and split the five gold bars with that person. They must have melted the bars and recast them to remove any proof of who previously owned them. The question in my mind is how big were the confederate gold bars. They may have been considerably bigger so the missing five bars could have been the equivalent of more than five bars of the size in the treasurers safe.

It appears that this gold may have belonged to the Confederacy, but was captured by the Union in 1864. The gold was then stolen from the Union. Since it was war time, it would seem that the rightful owners would be the United States government. Corporate Council was noncommittal on who owns the gold. He did say it belongs to the County now.

Were we prepared to let the full County Board of Supervisors deal with this? We are sure most think it belongs to the county since it was found on county forest property. Maybe they are right.

The County Board Chairman reported that the Veteran's Administrator of Pennsylvania has responded that maybe they would want Benjamin returned to that state for burial. They would need more time.

The full County Board meeting got underway. Some routine issues were dealt with and then the Forestry Committee Chairman reported on what they wanted done to allow people to visit Benjamin's den in an orderly and safe fashion. There were some questions about who would control the traffic, because the road is only one lane. The Chairman replied that they would hire off duty deputies, retired deputies and retired game wardens. It was explained that only about 20 vehicles at a time could drive to the temporary parking lot. They would have to leave before any other vehicles would be allowed in. No buses would be allowed. Yes, people could walk the one and one-half miles to the den. Parking at the trail head was also limited so some vehicles may have to park in the field across the highway. Permission has been granted to use that field.

The funds obtained from sale of the artifacts would be used to cover any expenses. The Forestry Chairman reported that two people with high quality metal detectors would sweep the area near the den. They would then sweep the entire forty acres. Our hope is that we may find where the victims of the booby trapped shotgun may be buried. Also, there may be things of interest that the metal detectors could find. A little more discussion and then a vote was taken - 16 ayes and 4 nays to allow the forestry plan to proceed.

Next came the discussion of what to do with the gold bars. Copies of the letter from Susan Ford were given to each board member. The Sheriff told of our telephone discussion with Ms. Ford. Then the questions started.

Are we sure we have recovered all the bars? We

tell that we are not sure, that is what the people with metal detectors may find, if there are some there, provided they are not too deep in the ground. Discussion continued. There was a strong feeling by many board members to claim it belongs to the county since it was found on county forest land. The Corporate Council agreed and since there are no marks on the gold bars, we really don't know the source of the gold. Maybe it was not the Confederate gold taken by Union soldiers at the Battle of the Wilderness in 1864.

One board member wanted to know if the value of the five gold bars had been determined. Each bar is very close to 13.7 pounds and at 16 ounces per pound that is about 220 ounces per bar at $1,000 per ounce. Each bar would be about $220,000 and there are five bars or about $1.1 million dollars.

More discussion was allowed and there seemed to be some sentiment to do some more investigating and see if there is some evidence to tie these gold bars to Benjamin. If we can not definitely make a connection, then perhaps we can take some appropriate action. There didn't seem to be any urgency with the board. Finally, a motion was made to postpone action on the gold bars until significant information is obtained. This motion passed on a 12 to 8 vote, as one member was absent.

The Sheriff brought in one of the rifles wrapped in skin, since they are now locked in the same room with the other artifacts other than coins, currency and gold bars. The Sheriff wanted the board to see what those guns were like. He unwrapped the gun and reported that is a .44-40 caliber. There are fourteen guns. We are not sure what the calibers of the others are. This one is an 1873 Winchester carbine with an octagon barrel.

We wanted some direction on disposing of these guns. Normally, the county sells excess property at a well advertised auction. A board member thought selling on eBay should be considered. We reported that the other two guns had been listed on eBay, mainly to get the loaded 10 gauge double barreled shotgun out of the county's liability. The last bid was over $1,800. The .44 rim fire 1864 Winchester carbine has a bid of over $1,500. Perhaps we should sell the carbine the same way as we decide to do the other carbines wrapped in skin. Finally, a motion was made to advertise the guns, and hold an auction in May of next year. The auction to be held in a large enough venue to handle a very large crowd. This motion passed by 16 to 4.

Thinking of those guns, I have collected ammunition since I was very young. There are well over 200 different calibers and shotgun shells in my collection. Some really old ones are a .45-85 and a .45-90. These calibers were from the post Civil War period. Other old shells are .38-55, .38-40, .25-20 and others. Gun powder from Benjamin G. Mason's era were black powder, and when a shot was fired a huge cloud of smoke was made. The powder, was also corrosive, so gun barrels needed to be cleaned after shooting. Of course, the modern guns need cleaning also.

Back to the board meeting. We reported that an advertisement was placed in appropriate sources to find an agent to dispose of the coins and currency. Because of the action today, the gold bars will not be sold yet. We are waiting for a response from the County Historical Society on their interest in the remaining artifacts. Perhaps anything not claimed by them could be offered for sale at the same time the rifles are offered.

On our request to bury Benjamin in the Northern Wisconsin Veteran's Cemetery, we were given approval. We asked the Wisconsin Veteran's Administration to ask their counterparts in Pennsylvania to see if they wanted Benjamin there and they are declining to give us an answer at this time. Perhaps Benjamin had fallen out of favor for reasons we may or may not ever find out.

During the citizen's comments portion at the end of the county board meeting, one person thanked the board for developing a good plan to allow people to visit this interesting place where Benjamin G. Mason had lived.

The plan to make a small parking lot halfway back to Benjamin's den was started immediately. The people with metal detectors went right to work. One thing we have not taken care of, is doing something about the hole under the tree top with the bayonet through the skull of the person that fell in the hole. That represents a dead body that needs to be properly identified, if possible, and properly buried.

Chapter 33

~~~~~

What happened around Hagerstown and Blue Ridge Summit during the Civil War seemed to haunt me. It appears as though General Leesome of the Confederates moved from Fredrick, Maryland to Hagerstown, Maryland in September 1862. Leesome wrote a letter to the people of Maryland trying to recruit men into the Confederate army from the Hagerstown area. This was the fall before the Gettysburg Battle a few miles away in Pennsylvania. Needless to say, very few Marylanders responded. It appears that only about 1,500 Marylanders were ever in the Confederate Army, even though Maryland is south of the Mason-Dixon Line and is considered a southern state.

Money was of great concern during the Civil War. General Keller of the Confederate Army demanded the City of Chambersburg in Pennsylvania turn over $100,000 in gold and $500,000 in greenbacks or the town would be burned. This happened in 1864 and the town refused, so it was burned. The town is just west of Gettysburg and Blue Ridge Summit.

I think that we have possibly put too much emphasis on Susan Ford's letter as far as trying to get to the reason that Lucy's brothers had such a strong dislike for Benjamin. It seems like the kind of feeling a feud brings out. Perhaps some, or all, of Lucy's brothers joined the Confederate Army, where as most Hagerstown volunteers joined Union Regiments.

Letters written by General Robert Leesome to the people of Hagerstown and Fredrick were very inflammatory. The letters were written in September 1862. From the time I heard of Lucy's brothers, I always thought it was hard feelings over the issue of the Civil War that was at the heart of the issue.

From what I have read, Benjamin G. Mason's troops did not ever fight Colonel Bradley Jackson, later Brigadier General Jackson, at any time. I don't doubt that the gold bars were stolen at the Battle of the Wilderness, and perhaps Benjamin and an accomplice did steal the five bars of gold. I don't think Lucy's brothers came to Benjamin's property to get the gold. They may not have even known about it.

As time goes on, we tend to continue thinking on sticky problems to try to get to the bottom of them. I began to wonder: What was Benjamin going to do with that gold? Benjamin arrived at his property about 1866. The last entry was for 1878. Benjamin lived on his property for about 12 years, and it may have been even longer.

He apparently did not have any big plans for the gold. He was getting older and it would seem that having a fortune in gold at his disposal would have prompted Benjamin to take the gold, turn it into cash and live someplace besides the den. With that gold, Benjamin could have come into a faraway city like, San Francisco, and live high on the hog. Maybe he had a plan to do something with the gold. Perhaps he had thieves remorse and realized that taking the gold was a very bad deed, something he later wished he had never done. Maybe he had plans to give it away to charity, poor relatives or maybe to Lucy's brothers to buy a truce.   That doesn't sound like Benjamin. Perhaps so much time had gone by that he really lost interest in the gold. He was getting along without it.

Chapter 34

Meanwhile, work on the parking lot was nearly finished. The people with the metal detectors were busy sweeping the area of the den. They did find some parts of horses bridles and some horse shoes. Benjamin did have a horse! I thought that in order to get his tools, utensils and sixty-eight pounds of gold to his property, he would have needed a horse, mule or oxen. These items will be turned over to the County Historical Society, if they want them.

The sweepers did find two pieces of native copper. Each piece weighed about a pound. These are pieces of pure copper, apparently carried by the last glacier. The copper probably came from the Upper Peninsula of Michigan. The metal detectors also turned up a broken tip of a slider hook on a log chain that was probably broken about 100 years ago. I wonder why Benjamin's den was not found then. Perhaps a large tree had fallen over the door and blocked it from view until other trees and brush could grow and protect the door from view.

After carefully sweeping the area, no evidence of human remains were found. We had thought perhaps a belt buckle, shoe nails, coins or something would trigger the detector. Maybe nobody got killed by the booby trapped gun. We know for sure someone died in the hole under the tree top. Maybe Benjamin took all the clothes, shoes, coins and anything not of flesh and blood, and took them faraway and buried them, or threw them away. He then buried a naked body and, unless they had gold fillings in their teeth, they would not trigger the detector from their graves. Not true with people living in today's world with fillings in their teeth, artificial knees and hips, pacemakers and other replacement parts of modern medicine.

That does solve one problem we thought we would have. What do we do about reburying Benjamin's victims? We still have to deal with the skull on the bayonet in the hole under the tree.

Tomorrow the road will be opened and manned to begin letting people back to visit Benjamin's den. We all hope it goes well. We do expect a great deal of interest, both from local people and others from far away.

Chapter 35

~~~~~

I got things ready and we chopped the corn for silage. My job is to push the silage up on the pile and pack it, as loads are brought in from the field and unloaded. This means more time to think, like all day to think!

We have lived on our property for 37 years. The people we bought the original farm from lived on the original 76 acres for forty years. They came from Rockford, Illinois during the depression and were looking for a place that they could raise their food. They raised five kids and they did not have running water in the house. They did have a water heater in the milk house, so warm water for doing dishes and taking baths was possible. This man was a World War I Veteran and was very short. He also walked with a limp from a war injury. The buildings he built had small, low doorways and until I got all of those buildings torn down, I had a bruised head from banging my head on the door casings. Their five children all went to college and somehow that family made it work for forty years.

Today, we own 235 acres and on that property are three other home sites of long ago. All had small basements under some small building. We often wonder who, when and what happened that they moved away. We do know that one house burned. Perhaps, people living like Benjamin did, was not that uncommon in a world far different than what we see today.

This county was not platted until 1915 when the first plat book was printed and the township of Beaver Brook was established. The first plat book shows nearly all of the property in our county was owned by individuals, not the state, county or federal government. With the depression and other factors, much of this land was lost for non-payment of taxes. The plat book now shows that over 30% of our county is owned by County, State and Federal owners. It is important to realize that every parcel of land in our county was transferred from the government for various reasons, by a patent, just like Benjamin received. Some people, like Benjamin, were rewarded for something they did. The railroads received huge tracts of land for building railroad tracks into this part of Wisconsin. Some tracts were rewarded for homesteading and others were sold to settlers, mainly immigrants from other countries. Today, land has become a very valuable possession and like the guy said, "they are not making anymore of it." Benjamin was one of the very first non-native people into this part of Wisconsin. The sad part is that the American Indians roamed and lived in this part of Wisconsin for hundreds of years and white people came along and took it from them. They did leave some small parcels, called reservations, for them to live in. Their lives, like the lives of many, many others were changed by 'progress'. This is very sad, but true!

Chapter 36

~~~~~

Our ad hoc committee decided we needed to meet so a meeting was set for next Tuesday. Again, there are several issues that need to be addressed. Meanwhile, one day I received a letter from Skokie, Illinois. It was from a Red Mason, a former basketball coach, and a man that I worked with one summer at a boys camp in our county. This was back in the 1960s. Mr. Mason claims that a pedigree that his father drew up shows a Benjamin G. Mason on their family tree, seven generations ago. Red said, "I am not claiming anything. Benjamin was a surveyor and lived near Hagerstown, Maryland." His father always said they were shirt tail (very shirt tail) relatives of the Masons of the Mason-Dixon Line surveyors. He continued that he was telling us this for our information. He knew that we were trying to figure things out.

Red Mason said that his family of Mason's are Irish. During the potato famine in Ireland, many of their clan living near Galway died. Some, however, did come to America. His father's information led him to believe that Benjamin came to America as a young man because of the potato famine in Ireland. Benjamin probably came to the

Hagerstown area because other relatives were living there. Red saw the program on television about Benjamin's den and was reminded of the time he and I skidded off the road during the 'great race' back to camp. Red was driving and we were ahead at that point. The letter was signed, thanks for finding Benjamin.

This seems to fit in with other Civil War information about the Irish. Benjamin must have moved to Blue Ridge Summit, Pennsylvania before the Civil War broke out. He volunteered to the 69th Pennsylvania Volunteer Infantry that was originally the 2nd Regiment, or Irish Brigade, 2nd Division Pennsylvania Militia. It was formed from several Militia groups, the Irish volunteers, Hibernian Greens and other militias. The vast majority of the 69th were Irish, or of Irish descent. They developed a very credible record, earning many battle ribbons throughout the duration of the Civil War. A Benjamin Mason apparently served with that Infantry and became a General.

Shortly after getting Red Mason's letter, I got a call from the County Historical Society. "You won't believe this," the director said. "We were examining Benjamin G. Mason's belongings and one of our group picked up a boot and was examining it. She found a pouch in the tongue of one of the leather boots. She worked with it and found a slip of paper in the pouch. We pulled it out and looked at it. It is a will, more or less. Seems like a very strange place to put a will."

"We carefully opened it," he continued, "and it was in remarkable condition. You and your committee need to see it." I thanked him and told him we would pick it up the next day.

What does that paper say? Our meeting was the next day and I could hardly wait. I picked up the boot with the paper tucked back in the tongue. Betty and I were very anxious, but we did not look at the paper and took it to our meeting.

The Chairman started the meeting. We should accept the latest bid for the double barreled shotgun. The latest bid was $1,941. We approved it, so the County Treasurer will accept that bid and carry out the transaction. It will be good to get that gun out of the County's jurisdiction.

Next, the Chairman reported that Pennsylvania Veteran's Administrator declined taking Benjamin's remains and giving him proper burial. The other news is that apparently now the Wisconsin Veteran's Administration has withdrawn their offer to bury Benjamin in the

Northern Wisconsin Veteran's Cemetery. It appears the suspicion of Benjamin and an accomplice stealing the five gold bars cast an ugly shadow over the entire request.

What should we do about a resting place for Benjamin? Maybe we should put him back in his den and lock the door. No way!! Hold on a minute. First of all, it may be illegal on county forest land. Second of all, it may not be a good idea because after the road is closed back to the den, vandalism could occur to the den. The County Forester said he will check to see if putting Benjamin back where he has been for at least 135 years is possible under State Statutes for county forests.

Next, we talked about not finding any bodies by the folks using the metal detectors. What do we do with the skull on the bayonet in the hole under the tree top? We all agreed that we need to do something. Discussion followed and in the end we decided to use the Forestry Department skid steer and carry two or three buckets full of gravel back there and fill in the hole. The tree top will have to be trimmed back to get at the hole. We all agreed.

Next, the boot was brought up. We gathered

around the boot and opened the pouch on the tongue. We pulled out the small piece of paper or skin. It was folded in half so we unfolded the paper and it read: *Gold Bars to Irish Charities. B. Mason June 1878.* Apparently Benjamin was feeling that the time had come to do something. This is around the time he heard the train whistle and walked toward it and found the workers building the limestone tunnel for the new railroad. Benjamin sent a telegram to Lucy, but did not receive a reply. Now the will is found dated from that same period of time. Now what! Just where are the Irish Charities located? Is there such an outfit?

When Betty got home from the meeting, she googled Irish Charities and would you believe there are a large number of them. As to be expected, there was a wide variety and many did not fit what we assumed Benjamin had in mind. Since he had seen the potato famine in Ireland, he saw first hand how people suffered and died. My feeling is that Benjamin wanted the gold to help relieve peoples, rather Irish peoples, suffering. It turns out that there is just such an Irish Charity in Hagerstown, Maryland called 'Doctors of Mercy'. Since it was listed as an Irish Charity it must serve primarily Irish people in need of medical assistance. We know that Benjamin lived in

Hagerstown when he came from Ireland. Any decision about gold would first have to be handled by the ad hoc committee and then approved by the full County Board.

News stories of Benjamin's den seem to have run their course and those people involved are finding their lives returning to a more normal pace. People wanting to visit the den have slowed to a trickle and rifle deer season is on the horizon. The Forestry Committee has planned to close the den several days before deer season.

The full County Board meets on the 2nd Tuesday in November and it is a day time meeting. It primarily deals with the annual county budget. If we want to do something with Benjamin's body, we should get some direction from the County Board. Also, we need to decide what will happen to the gold bars. Should the ad hoc committee meet before the full County Board meeting, or should we wait until later in the winter. The gold is not going anywhere and neither is Benjamin. The mortuary has already told us it will keep Benjamin for as long as needed. Nothing was said about what the charges will be. Maybe the County Board Chairman should ask the mortician about the cost, especially if he remains in the mortuary until spring.

We have received several proposals from our request for bids to dispose of the coins and currency. We do need to review the bids and choose someone. The Chairman of the ad hoc committee calls a meeting for next Thursday. OOPS! If we are going to review bids, perhaps the bidders should be invited. We also need to inform bidders that the gold bars will not be sold. The meeting is reset for the first Thursday in December. This will be after deer season, which around northern Wisconsin means many people hunt, or at least attempt to. Normal life during deer season just doesn't happen for many people. It is a big event. We will also invite the County Historical Society to come to the meeting.

Deer Season. This means I really have time to think. I sit in a 'deer observatory' built on poles about 12 feet off the ground. It is in one of our woods. Very little happens, but when there is action, it is really exciting. I see a lot of chickadees, nuthatches and squirrels. I have hunted nearly 60 seasons and have harvested 20 bucks. You can tell that there are a lot of years that I come home empty handed, but I still enjoy it. The sight of a mature white tailed buck is a beautiful sight to behold. It is guaranteed to raise your pulse rate. This year I watched a flock of about 30 wild turkeys during parts of several days of hunting.

I spent a large amount of time thinking about how we could reinforce Benjamin's den so we could put his remains back in the den and not have it collapse on him. The big wooden beams supporting the roof are strong, but eventually they will give out.

I have an idea that steel I-beams could be cut to the correct length for each of the eight wooden beams. A steel girder jack could be placed on a concrete pad and under the I-beam, up under the large wooden beams. They could be welded in place also. Heavy triangle plates could be put in between the steel beams and held in place by a girder jack or two. This should provide great support for the roof of the den. We can discuss this idea, or others, during our December meeting. Hopefully by then, the County Forester will have found out if Benjamin can be buried on county forest property. I hope it will be approved as it now seems to be the logical and fitting place for Benjamin G. Mason. After all, he already has been lying there for over 135 years.

We have separated our calves from their mothers. We gave them all their shots and by now everyone has accepted the fact that they are not going to be together so they have stopped their bellowing and bawling. It is much more peaceful.

When we were through working the calves, we realized that we were one calf short. We knew we already lost one nice bull calf in late summer. We are nearly positive it was killed by timber wolves, as several were seen in that part of the pasture where the calf died. He was nearly entirely eaten. We are very suspicious that the missing calf probably was killed by timber wolves also.

We are just ordinary people and finding Benjamin's den has caused our lives to become very full for a few months. We sense that we are heading down the home stretch and hope it all turns out alright. We must get ready for the December ad hoc committee meeting.

I received a letter from a man in Philadelphia requesting a sample of Benjamin's hair. This will have to be discussed at the December meeting. I hope that doesn't mean trouble. Why would the man want a lock of Benjamin's hair? Is it a potential relative? At first glance, I am not in favor of sending this man any hair. Maybe he will get a court order, but I hope not. Perhaps this person wants to do a DNA search on Benjamin's hair. I have not done any research on who could do it, when or how expensive, at all. I know it can be done and apparently is very accurate if a good sample is obtained.

Chapter 37

~~~~~

Deer season passes and life returns to a more or less normal pace. I really enjoy hunting, but after nine days, I am glad I don't have to hunt any more.

The December meeting of the ad hoc committee is called to order by the Chairman. First on the agenda is picking someone to sell the currency and coins for the county. Since the gold bars will not be sold, only two people showed up to present their program. We had samples of the coins and currency with the number of each that we wanted sold.

We met with each presenter separately. Both were very capable presenters and their plan to find buyers were somewhat similar. Both would use the internet and report to the County Treasurer. We wanted all transactions to be done by the 11th of May, which is a Saturday. An inventory of the coins and currency would be made by the Treasurer and a refundable certified check equal to the appraisal of the coin and currency, plus 25%, similar to a security bond, would be required. The appraisal would be done by an independent broker. The winning bidder would be able to take the coins and have them in their possession until they are sold by May 11th. Bids were presented and one broker would charge 9% of the total sales. The other broker would charge 11% of the total sale. Being a quasi governmental committee, we took the offer for 9%. The contract would commence by presenting a Security Bond Certified Check to the County Treasurer.

Next, the County Historical Society was on the agenda. This hard working group had looked at all the tools, utensils, compass, surveyors chain, clothes, boots and traps. They would be happy to take all of the items. We had the two gold watches and the sheath knife. We had not put them with either the currency and coins, or the things for the County Historical Society. We made a motion to include the two watches and knife with the other things for the Historical Society. I said, "Motion to accept County Historical Society's offer." Motion seconded and passed by all. Many thanks for helping out. Next on the agenda is dealing with Benjamin's gold.

Chapter 38

~~~~~

We discuss the will like note found in one of Benjamin's boots where he requested the gold go to the Irish Charities. Since he had lived at Hagerstown, Maryland when he apparently came from Ireland back to the United States, it seemed logical to look there. Betty found an Irish Charity in Hagerstown, Maryland called Doctors of Mercy. We have an address. Much discussion followed. The Board Chairman felt very strong sentiment for the County keeping it since it was found on County Forest property. We all agreed that it was the way the meeting seemed to go when the gold was discussed. This note puts a different view on the matter. We finally vote, and all approve presenting the idea of the gold going to the Irish Charities with the ad hoc committee recommendation that we do that.

We do not expect that recommendation to go over very well. It would not be easy to let $1.1 million, or more, slip through their hands. That would look good on the bottom line for the county budget. The next agenda item was what do we do with Benjamin's remains. We already know that the Veterans Administration of both Pennsylvania and

Wisconsin are not interested in having Benjamin interred with them. We had briefly discussed possibly putting Benjamin back in the den. We needed to know what the County Forester found in the State Statutes. His report was good news. He found no Statute that would prohibit Benjamin's being buried on county forest land. The Corporate Council concurred.

We discussed the pros and cons of putting Benjamin G. Mason's remains back in the den and sealing it. We all agreed that it was the best place for Benjamin, since he had already been there for at least 135 years.

I presented my idea about using I-beams, girder jacks and other steel to reinforce the roof. We also need to put some sort of fence around the den so people, or machines, like log skidders, will not be able to get on the roof of the den. The chimney needs to be blocked with concrete also.

We agreed to put a headstone beside the door. We will decide what goes on the head stone at a later date. Nothing will be done until spring anyway. We also agreed to put up a heavy steel grate in front of the door so it is still visible. This would be set in a large amount of concrete. We all agreed on this plan and will ask the full County Board to approve it at the same time we try to resolve the issue with the gold bars.

I brought up the request for a hair sample from the person in Philadelphia. Discussion followed and no one was in favor of us doing this. Corporate Council said that the county does not have the authority to give up any of Benjamin's hair without a court order. I gave Corporate Council the letter and asked him to please contact this person with our response. He agreed. What if a court says we need to give this person some hair. If it happens before he is buried that is OK. After he is buried, not so good. Perhaps we need to snip some of Benjamin's hair, keep it in the County Treasurers safe just in case. We all agreed.

We need to develop a plan to advertise the fifteen guns and the many boxes of ammunition that will be for sale in May. Perhaps we should talk to some public relations firms and see what advice they could offer. The County Board Chairman offered to do this soon.

It appears like we are ready for the December full County Board meeting. We remind the County Board Chairman to put these issues on the agenda for the December meeting. Also, to consult with Corporate Council for exact wording on dealing with the gold bars. It was postponed at an earlier meeting.

We were about to adjourn when the Sheriff suggested that we cremate Benjamin's remains and scatter them near the den. This would eliminate getting a head stone. Also, we should rethink keeping the den by reinforcing it. The Forester said he thought his committee would be in favor of removing any liability for the County. Perhaps we could ask to remove the roof, leave the fireplace and rock walls intact. A chain link fence could be built around, and over, the remains of the den. The fence should also be extended to include the tunnel. Since this is a place of interest, we should try to preserve some of it.

Discussion followed, and we decided to amend our recommendation to the County Board. We would ask to cremate Benjamin G. Mason and scatter his ashes near the den. We would remove the roof and install a chain link fence around, and over, the remains of the den and tunnel. Everyone agreed. The County Forestry Committee meets the week before the full county board meets. The Forester will put these items on the agenda and hopefully get approval. Meeting was adjourned.

Chapter 39

~~~~~

The December full County Board meeting gets started. Visitor comments are heard and are from a wide range of issues, like usual. The Board works through the agenda until the items involving Benjamin are next. The County Board Chairman reported that a broker has been selected to dispose of the currency and coins. An independent broker appraised them at $34,650 plus 25% that is what the Certified Check in the Treasurers office is for. When the currency and coins are sold by May 11th, the county will pay a 9% commission to the broker when he turns over the revenue he has collected, along with a list of each item sold and the price paid for it. The broker would get the certified check back.

The County Board Chairman reported that the County Historical Society will take all the utensils, tools, compass, surveyor's chain, traps and clothes. The ad hoc committee also gave the two gold watches and the sheath knife to the County Historical Society. Their chairman was present and was very appreciative to receive the items mentioned. Many pictures of the den were taken as well, and given to the Historical Society.

The question of what to do with the five gold bars, whose current value was about $1.4 million, was discussed. The Chairman reported that a will, of sorts, was found in a pouch in the tongue of one of Benjamin's boots. The County Historical Society crew discovered it. It was a small slip of paper, or skin, and it said, *Gold to Irish Charities. B. Mason, 1878.*

Benjamin apparently lived in America when he fought in the Indian Wars. He received the 40 acres in exchange for that service, in a patent, signed by President Martin Van Buren, 1839. He apparently returned, or went to Ireland, in the early 1840s. The Irish Potato Famine occurred from 1845 to 1850. Over one million Irish died and over one million migrated to other countries.
  Apparently that is when Benjamin came to Hagerstown, Maryland, very close to the town of Blue Ridge Summit, Pennsylvania where he lived before fighting in the Indian Wars. What he did for many years is not known, but he did come to this land in our county around 1866. Benjamin died sometime after June of 1878.

We already know that property found on county forest property belongs to the County. However, the ad hoc committee is recommending that the five gold bars be given to the Irish Charities of

Hagerstown, Maryland, which is known as Doctors of Mercy.

The County Board Chairman said he will make that motion. According to the County's rules of Order, which includes Roberts Rules of Order, no discussion on a motion can be made unless it is seconded. The chairman called for a second of his motion. No one offered a second. He asked for a second again and a third time. No second was made to the motion. The Board Chairman said that, "The motion dies for lack of a second."

The Chairman of the Forestry Committee asked to speak and made the motion for the county to keep possession of the five gold bars and develop a plan to sell them. This should be all done by the May County Board meeting. The Chairman asked if there was a second and several board members offered. One member did second the motion. Now discussion could begin.

One board member said, "It is clear to me. The gold was on our property, so it is ours to do with what we want." Another board member said, "Finding the paper with Benjamin desiring the gold to go to Irish Charities makes the issue somewhat clouded." Discussion continued, and there definitely was the feeling by some to give the gold to Irish Charities.

Finally, a board member made a motion to move the question, which cut off discussion and required a vote on the motion before the body. The request was for a signed paper ballot. The County Clerk passed out ballots and the vote took place. The ballots were counted and those in favor of the motion 11, and those opposed 10. The Chairman reported that the motion to retain the five gold bars passed. He told the board to take a short break before proceeding.

In the County's Rules of Order, a board member voting on the prevailing side can ask for a revote of a motion. That motion must be seconded by another board member. When the board reconvened, a member voting for the motion asked for a revote. The ballots were checked and the person requesting a revote had voted for the motion for the county to keep the gold.

After the motion was seconded, the Chairman asked for discussion. The supervisor making the motion said, "Maybe we could keep part of the gold and give part to Irish Charities." He said, "I would suggest splitting the gold."

The Chairman called for a revote of the motion for the county to keep the gold. Again a signed paper ballot was used. The Clerk collected ballots and counted them. This time the vote was yes 7, and no 14. The motion failed. Now the Chairman asked them if there were any other motions on this subject. The supervisor requesting a revote made a new motion to split the gold by the May board meeting. This time a roll call vote was taken and that motion passed 18 yes and 3 no. This seemed like a good compromise, and the ad hoc committee was pleased with it.

Next, the Chairman explained that a publicity agent was going to be hired to advertise the sale of the 15 guns and the boxes of ammunition, which would be done at the May 11th county surplus and land sale. It is anticipated that these old guns and ammunition will be well sought after.

The Board Chairman brought up giving Benjamin a final resting place. He asked the Forestry Committee Chairman to make a presentation to the board. He told of the idea of cremating the remains and spreading the ashes near the den. He explained about removing the roof of the den, putting a chain link fence around and over the remains of the den and tunnel. He also reported that the Forestry Committee had approved that plan and made the motion to accept the plan as presented. The motion was seconded and discussion was called for.

"Was cremating by the county legal?" asked a

supervisor. Corporate Council said, "It probably was, but in this case there appears to be no next of kin to approve it. I think you should go ahead and vote pending approval from the State Attorney General's office." Motion was amended, seconded and passed. The amended motion, seconded and voted and passed 21-0. Now the ball is in the State Attorney General's office. Corporate Council will present our case.

Chapter 40

~~~~~

It is January and it is time to sell the feeder cattle. We hire a big cattle semi truck called a 'pot'. It is called this because it is a Double Decker to haul feeders. They will go to a big sale in southern Minnesota near the Iowa border. This particular sale is in conjunction with the Midwest Auctioneer Contest and about 2500 to 3000 feeders will be sold. Betty and I always go and watch our beauties get sold and go to new homes.

The sale was very well attended, over 100 buyers from several states. Feeders are divided into steers and heifers, and then grouped according to size. Ours are eligible for purchase by overseas buyers and they perform very well in the sales ring. We are happy to have a good reputation among the buyers.

While looking up something on the genealogy of my mothers relatives, I make an amazing discovery. My great, great, great grandfather was married to a Hannah Mason. Not only that, but her father was Benjamin Mason! His grandfather was also named Benjamin Mason! Could Hannah Mason have had a brother named Benjamin Mason? The dates of her life are from 1783 to 1850. Her family lived at Swansea, Massachusetts and when married, Hannah moved to Rehoboth, Massachusetts.

Families long ago seemed to be spread out with great differences in ages. It may have been to keep help around the house or business to make life easier for the parents. Also, other relatives had come from Ireland in the late 1700s and early 1800s.

These relatives lived in Massachusetts and Pennsylvania near the Maryland border. Perhaps our Benjamin G. Mason had migrated from Massachusetts to Pennsylvania or Maryland as a young man. We know he fought in the Indian Wars and was rewarded the 40 acres in Wisconsin in 1839. He must have been at least 16 then, and maybe much older. Maybe he was 20 years old in 1839. That would make him being born in 1819. Hannah Mason was born in 1783 and would have been 36 years old when Benjamin was born. Not improbable. The records available to me don't go any further then what is written here. Perhaps it is a dead end. After all, Mason is not an uncommon name.

Reading further, several of my mothers relatives died or were injured in the Civil War. One died in the second Battle of Bull Run, one died on May 5th at the Wilderness, and another was wounded and taken prisoner in the Battle of the Peninsula in June of 1862. Another was taken prisoner and later died in the confederate prison at Andersonville. It appears that my mothers ancestors were willing to defend their beliefs even if it required them to bear arms. Maybe that was what inspired Benjamin to serve under Captain Billy in the Indian Wars, or maybe it was something exciting to do for a young man. Or maybe he could escape some distasteful situation at home. Maybe it was family, maybe it was his peers. I doubt if we will ever know.

Chapter 41

~~~~~

The County Corporate Council got an opinion from the State Attorney General's office. It said that in this unique case, the county would have to advertise for permission from the next of kin in order to cremate the remains of the deceased. The county must wait for 60 days. If no next of kin comes forward, the county can cremate the body in question.

About that same time, Corporate Council received a reply from the man in Philadelphia. It was a Court Order requiring the county to provide a sample of Benjamin's hair. It was to be shipped by Federal Express to an address in Philadelphia. I was getting the feeling that the man requesting the hair sample was a Philadelphia lawyer, a phrase common when I was a kid.

Why did this man want the hair sample? For DNA testing? For what? To see if they were related? Or some other sinister plan, unknown to myself and probably any other people in our county? Was this man after Benjamin's estate? Maybe the gold bars? I wonder if this comes down to a full fledged court fight and this man has a valid claim to kinship, would the county prevail.

A meeting of the ad hoc committee was called to order. Corporate Council reported on the two recent events. Since we were a quasi governmental committee, we had posted our agenda in the proper places.

The Chairman made a motion to, "suspend the rules". It was seconded and passed with no dissenting votes. This allowed free discussion without a motion being made and seconded. Much discussion followed. It appears that the court order must be complied with. Our committee was indignant about the court order. Was it legitimate? Corporate Council said it was the real deal and we would be asking for trouble if we refused to comply. What was the motivation? Finally, it was agreed to send a letter to the Philadelphia lawyer and tell him he would have to meet with our committee before we would comply with the courts order. A motion was made to return to the agenda and it passed. A motion was made, and passed unanimously, to send the letter.

Regarding the Attorney General's opinion, it was discussed and seemed like a reasonable opinion. We agreed that we should advertise in our local papers, wait 60 days and then cremate Benjamin G. Mason's remains. We discussed what should be in the advertisement. Finally, we decided to tell it like it was. *In the matter of Benjamin G. Mason, the County is in possession of his remains and wants to cremate him and scatter his ashes near his den in the county forest. Any next of kin, with verifiable proof there of, should contact the County with plans to care for Benjamin's remains. This needs to be done within sixty days, or by March 21st. Contact the County Sheriff.*

Chapter 42

~~~~~

In early February, I receive a letter from Susan Ford, the military history buff from Hagerstown, Maryland. She had good access to ships manifests that listed passengers coming to America. Low and behold, she said she found a Benjamin G. Mason arriving at Boston on the Brigatine 'Albion' from St. Johns, Newfoundland on September 7, 1848. He, and 36 others, had come from Ireland to St. Johns on the 'Robert Burns', 247 tons, from Londonderry, Ireland. The group had left Ireland because of the Great Potato Famine from 1845 to 1852. Over one million people starved to death and over one million migrated to other countries, mostly to the United States.

Also, in the group with Benjamin was a family by the name of Boyd. William was the father, his wife was Margaret. They came from County Down in Ireland. Also listed in the family were Caleb, age 32, Martin, age 30, Lucy, age 29 and Richard, age 23. Benjamin G. Mason's age listed him as 29, also from County Down in Ireland.

Could this be the Lucy that Ben had gotten the letters from? One gold watch had Caleb, 1861 engraved on the back. What about Martin and Richard. Could these men all have been victims of Benjamin's booby trapped gun and pit? Did something happen on the ships coming from Ireland to America?

Are these two families related? Is it a family feud? Were Benjamin and Lucy lovers at one time? Where did these people go when they came to America? Benjamin was a surveyor at one time. Was that before he went to Ireland, or after he returned? Maybe he worked as a surveyor in Ireland. I do know that the English were very active in Ireland about the time of the potato famine. They purchased large amounts of land, removed tenants from the land and planted crops like wheat. When we visited Ireland, we saw the remnants of several homes that the people living there had died during the great potato famine. These homes were very small and made out of rock, except for the roof.

No wonder Benjamin built his den out of rocks and made it very small. Conditions in Ireland at the time Benjamin left must have been disastrous. There was great social upheaval in response to many tenants being thrown off their land. Secret organizations were formed to reply to this outrage. Groups like the Rightboys, Thrashers and others protested the action by the English. Perhaps Benjamin and the Boyd boys were part of one of these organizations involved in midnight raids against the English. These events apparently happened just before the Great Potato Famine.

Chapter 43

~~~~~

It appears that the Boyd's and Benjamin G. Mason came from County Down, sailed on the same ship to America, and probably knew each other. What did these people do from 1848 to 1861, when the Civil War began. Where did they live? At least we are fairly certain that the Boyd's lived in, or around, Hagerstown, Maryland. Benjamin lived around Blue Ridge Summit, Pennsylvania. What about Lucy? By the start of the war she could have been 42 years old. Maybe she and Benjamin had been lovers and the brothers deemed Benjamin was not good enough for their sister. Something bad must have happened to cause this great anger by Lucy's brothers. It could go way back to County Down in Ireland.

The events at The Wilderness may be what it is all about, also. Benjamin's troops killing some fellow union soldiers by friendly fire and the gold being stolen from the Confederates with it looking like Benjamin and an accomplice took it. If only we had a time machine to look back, but we don't. We can only try to piece together bits and pieces of history to help us understand exactly what happened.

Chapter 44

~~~~~

Our County Corporate Council received a reply from the Philadelphia lawyer. The lawyer was in a state of high agitation. He had no plans to come to our county to get a sample of Benjamin's hair. What is the reason the hair can not be sent? The court order was clear. We must provide him with some hair. This time he included a phone number, so Corporate Council called him.

The lawyer was pleasant on the telephone. He explained that he was an amateur historian for the 69th Pennsylvania. Part of his responsibility is to collect an artifact from each of the soldiers of the 69th since it was made up of many Irish Militias and other Irish from Philadelphia and other Pennsylvania towns. He said, "We feel Philadelphia is home to the 69th. We have artifacts from 879 soldiers out of the 901 soldiers that were ever assigned duty in the 69th. Brigadier General Benjamin G. Mason is one of the last 22 soldiers of the 69th that we do not have any artifact from. All I am requesting is a lock of hair to fill in a tribute to the soldiers of the 69th."

Why didn't he tell us that in his letter? Corporate

Council thought that if this lawyer could verify what he wanted the hair for, we could send it to him. We still wonder if it is a ruse to get the hair to take a DNA sample from it.

Then again, would they have any DNA from Benjamin to compare it to? We certainly don't want someone to show up waving a handful of DNA data claiming they were a relative of Benjamin. Since so much time has passed it could be hard to prove if they were kin to Benjamin. It would be time consuming and I expect it would require the county to hire an outside attorney. Corporate Council will email the Philadelphia lawyer and ask for some verification.

Chapter 45

~~~~~

I got to thinking that if this Philadelphia lawyer was a historian for the 69th, maybe he knows more about the gold captured at The Wilderness. I called and asked him that question. He said, "He knew about the gold, but could not recall all the facts. He asked for a little time and to call back in two days."

I called him two days later and the 69th Pennsylvania historian was ready. He told me, "The Wilderness battle had just begun on May 5, 1864. Troops were still being positioned. A picket for General Mason's brigade was posting on a sunken road on the right flank of the main battle group. A single wagon with four horses came from the west. The driver was not in uniform of any army. The picket challenged the driver, wanting to stop his progress as he was headed directly into the main body of Union troops."

"The picket stepped out onto the road and signaled for the driver to stop. The driver snapped the reins and the horses accelerated, nearly running the picket over. As the wagon went by the picket, suddenly several Confederate Soldiers rose up from the bed of the wagon. They raised their guns as the wagon sped away. They shot at the picket, but because of the moving wagon, all shots missed the picket."

He continued, "The picket got off a shot and hit the driver who dropped the reins and fell off the wagon, apparently dead. The horses now had no one holding the reins and they continued down the sunken road in a runaway fashion. In a short while, the horse and wagon ran right into General Mason's brigade. The horses veered sharply away from the surprised troops. The horses ran off the road and into a dense thicket and then into a swamp. The wagon tipped over as the horses tried to avoid the swamp, and the Confederate Soldiers in the wagon got spilled into the swamp. The Union Soldiers began firing and since the Confederate guns were empty, it was not much of a contest. They all were killed. The horses were captured and controlled. The wagon was demolished and about that time the Confederate troops near that scene, charged the Union troops. They also were about a brigade strength. The Union troops repulsed the charge and dug in as did the Confederates. The Wilderness was rightly named, as it was a battlefield of very dense vegetative growth, mature trees and swampy wet conditions."

"The battle raged for hours and finally the Union troops could move forward as the Confederates retreated. Eventually, the wreck of the wagon was behind the Union line. The battle raged on and after a short time, the Confederates made a stand as night approached. Pickets were posted, troops took time to dig holes, move logs to make breast works and generally prepare to stay for the night."

He also said, "The Commanders were behind the front lines and finally someone went to inspect the wreck of the wagon. It was laying on its side in about two feet of mud and water. The contents were strewn around. Mainly food, coats, straw and parts of the wagon. There also were parts of a heavy wooden box about two feet long, sixteen inches wide and sixteen inches high. The contents of the box had fallen out and presumably was in the water."

"What might have happened is that General Mason and another officer, being behind and away from the other troops, went to the wreck and investigated it. They probably realized the heavy box had held gold bars and was on its way to Richmond, which was the Confederate capitol. They waded into the water and indeed found some gold bars. Perhaps, being by themselves, they took five gold bars and buried them in a spot that they could find when the war ended. None of this was confirmed. No one came forward claiming to have witnessed this event."

"So", he said, "General Mason now sought out a runner to an officer in the front to send six soldiers to his location. The soldiers were told to prepare to get wet and muddy. They were instructed to begin looking for gold bars. The soldiers began and immediately found gold bars. They brought them out of the mud and water and piled them on dry land. By now it was nearly dark. Several guards were posted around the gold."

"Shortly after nightfall, General Mason gave the order to load the gold bars onto a Union freight wagon and take it to a spot about one mile from the front lines. A hastily dispatched group of 40 soldiers were assigned duty to guard the gold for the night. Several fires were lit, and kept going all night, to provide light to see any Confederates that may try to take the gold back. It is doubtful that the Confederates knew about the gold since all men in the wagon were killed and movements of gold were always of strict secrecy."

"The gold bars were counted and there were 27. The men who searched and found the bars could not be certain they had indeed found all the gold bars. They were instructed to search again at first light. The next morning, these men found three more bars, bringing the total to 30 gold bars."

He told us, "The gold was moved to Washington. One hundred Union Soldiers and twenty Calvary guarded the gold and it arrived safely. The war ended a little over a year later."

"After the war, General Curtiss, of the defeated Confederate Army, indicated that, the capture of the 35 gold bars at The Wilderness was a significant blow to the Confederacy. Funds were badly needed by the south, especially then."

"Let's just wait a minute," I said, "Someone in Washington said that only 30 gold bars were captured and taken to Washington." The lawyer said, "Certainly General Curtiss was mistaken. However, he insisted he was correct, even though he had not actually seen the gold."

"The war was over, but the department of the Army felt compelled to investigate the discrepancy of the gold bars. General Mason was called to testify and he told the assembled body about the terrible conditions when the wagon had tipped. Even though his troops searched time and time again, it might be possible that the gold is still there, deep in the mud of the swamp."

He continued, "General Mason suggested that in case no one had thought of it, perhaps the men delivering the gold had taken the bars, hidden them to be found later and divided up between them. No shipping manifest was ever found, or offered, by the Confederates. What would they do now, anyway, they lost the war and after all to the victor goes the spoils."

"The investigators thanked General Mason and concluded that there was a possibility that the bars were stolen before the wreck in The Wilderness. This is the only slight blemish on Brigadier General Mason's fine record. He returned to Blue Ridge Summit, however he did not stay long and literally disappeared."

The 69th historian had not heard of General Masons whereabouts until the wonderful story of our finding him in his den.

Chapter 46

~~~~~

March means it is time to give the beef cows their annual shots that protect them from several diseases. These shots also develop immunity in their unborn calves, which will start to be born in April.

April arrives and it is hard to break free of winters grip on some days, but beginning to get warm with many more hours of daylight. Arrival of the calves means checking often to see if any cows need assistance with the birth. It also means getting up during the night to check on them. Most calves are born without assistance, but difficult births can happen. If it is a cold, windy day, the newborn calf needs protection to get dried off. A hair drier can be a big help. The sight of a newborn calf is exciting. I really like kneeling down and putting my arm around a new baby calf.

A publicity firm has been engaged to promote the sale of the fifteen guns and ammunition that will be sold at the county's excess property sale on May 11th. The Philadelphia lawyer has indeed proven trustworthy so a lock of Benjamin G. Mason's hair has been sent to him and the rest of the 69th Pennsylvania history committee. Some of Benjamin's hair is left in the safe.

The currency and coins sale is underway and is also to be completed by May 11th. We are certainly very curious as to how those articles are being received. The advertisement for notification by next of kin expired on March 21st. No one came forward, so our ad hoc committee has called a meeting to proceed with the process of cremating Benjamin and any other matters needing attention, such as the sale of the gold bars.

The ad hoc committee convened and discussed the procedure for the cremation of Benjamin. The mortuary will take care of it, but they need a signature to approve the procedure. Discussion followed. It was suggested that perhaps I could sign since there is a possibility Benjamin could be related to me. While it may be true, it may also not be true. I guess I really didn't want to find out. That may seem strange, but reconnecting with a relative from so long ago seemed confusing to me. On one hand, I am very curious, and on the other hand I wonder what would my responsibility be if Benjamin were related to me. I would feel compelled to notify my relatives on my Mothers side, which would certainly not be difficult and would be good to reconnect, or connect with younger folks.

If we were related, perhaps we could claim to be heirs to his estate. Not knowing all my relatives, there could be someone with the knowledge, funds and desire to challenge the countys claim to Benjamin's estate. That could get to be a real sticky wicket and after long and careful thought, I have resisted getting a DNA match done for the reasons listed. I do, however, feel an attraction to, and respect for, Benjamin. I have also considered finding out if we are related because of respect for my mothers relatives who came to eastern Massachusetts in the mid 1500s. My mother always claimed she was English/Scottish/Irish. Her relatives were among the earliest immigrants to America. One of my relatives was married to John D. Rockefeller's sister before he formed Standard Oil.

This decision did not come easy, and I thanked the committee for considering my signature, but I declined. We then concluded that the County Board Chairman should sign the release so Benjamin could be cremated. It would be done by the end of April.

The Committee then took up the sale of the gold

bars. We decided to let the County Treasurer transact that sale. The County Board Chairman had done some checking on how we would actually complete the sale. He had contacted two firms that deal with precious metals. One in San Francisco and the other in New York City. The process is about the same for both firms. We would commit the gold bars to them, they would assay them to determine the purity of the gold. We would ship the bars to them through the U. S. Postal Service.

Once the bars have been assayed, both companies said they would make an offer to purchase based on the price on the New York Mercantile Exchange, called the Spot Price. We would have a short time to accept or reject their bid. We would have to pay storage fees if the price was rejected. The San Francisco firm has an agent in Milwaukee, Wisconsin. The New York firm does not.

The committee approves the San Francisco firm. The Board Chairman will contact the County Treasurer and proceed. Hopefully the sale can be completed soon.

Chapter 47

~~~~~

Many calves have been born and we have had good luck. I really like the newborn calves. Some of the mothers can be very protective. There were no difficult births and we have no losses. There were two sets of twins that have been born so far. These always require keeping the mother and the twins confined together with no other animals for at least two weeks. Generally the mother favors one twin over the other. The two week rule works good. One year we had four sets of twins born on our farm.

An older stand of alfalfa needs to be replaced. Last fall, lime was spread on the field according to soil tests. Spraying was done to kill off the old vegetation. By mid April, I rent a No Till seeder and reseed the field to alfalfa and timothy grass. This means no open soil to erode and much less fuel and time spent preparing the soil. Around here we have a fair amount of rocks left from the last glacier. They melted about 11,000 years ago leaving rocks and debris that had been picked up on the way south. Around our farm, we try to be good stewards of the land. We are only temporarily using it and have a huge responsibility to treat it very carefully. Anyone using the land in the future will have at least the same opportunities that we have had.

Chapter 48

~~~~~

May 11th is here and the county has rented the Civic Center, the largest room in the county. It is a hockey arena, but the ice has been removed as some maintenance needed to be done.

The auction of land parcels begins at 10:00 a.m. These are parcels that the owners, failed to pay taxes on. Some years there are 20 or more parcels. This year there are only 12 and bidding is brisk.

Next comes the sale of surplus office equipment, furniture and miscellaneous tools. The highway department has some equipment not needed, as does the forestry department. Bidding gets done on these items by 11:45 a.m. Now it is time for the guns.

A special auctioneer has been procured by the publicity firm as part of their contract with the county.

The guns and ammunition have been displayed on one end of the arena. Each gun has a placard telling make, model and caliber of the gun. The skin wrapped around each gun went with each of the fourteen found in the fur traders basement. Benjamin's gun did not have the skin and it was to be sold first. There was a huge crowd of prospective buyers and curiosity seekers. Buyers interested in bidding for the guns had to register and be given a bidding number.

The rules for bidding were explained. Payment would be required before removal of the guns. A 6% auctioneers fee would be added to each bid to cover expenses. Buyers registration showed buyers from at least eleven states.

The first gun was brought out. This was Benjamin's 1864 Winchester lever action .44 caliber rim fire. Apparently this was a very rare gun. The auctioneer started the bidding at $10,000! That was an eye opener! It quickly got raised, and raised. It finally sold for $21,550. To think my Uncle Doug had one just like it, and he was cleaning closets one day in the 1950s and threw it out. Too bad!

The first of the remaining skin wrapped guns was to be sold next. The auctioneer started at $20,000. Bidding rapidly went up to $34,600 and was sold at that price. One after another, the guns were sold. It took one and one-half hours to sell all fifteen guns. The boxes of ammunition were sold next. There were 39 boxes that averaged $149 per box. The total gross sale was $494,061. Bidders would have to have paid another $29,295 for auctioneers fees. Our expenses for the auctioneer and publicity firm was $50,000, leaving a profit of $444,061 to go into the countys treasury. How it will be appropriated will be decided later.

The date of May 11th was when the sale of coins and currency was to be completed. The firm getting the bid, contacted the County Treasurer and wanted to meet her at 3:00 p.m. at the treasurers office. Since this was on a Saturday, it required a trip to the office for the Treasurer, but she agreed.

At 3:00 p.m., the broker for the coins and currency arrived. Several of us on the ad hoc committee went from the sale of the guns to the Treasurers office. The broker reported that the coins and currency went very well. He first produced an inventory and price of each item. He then produced a certified check for $151,250 and gave it to the County Treasurer. She in turn gave him back his security check for $42,500. The Treasurer then wrote out a commission check of $13,613, or 9% commission on the total sale. This means another $137,637 into the County Treasury.

The Treasurer had completed negotiations with the San Francisco precious metals firm to ship the gold to San Francisco via U.S. Postal Service, registered mail with return receipt requested. The precious metals firm will hire an assay firm to determine its purity. The firm will then make the County Treasurer an offer which we can accept or reject. The five gold bars weigh about 13.72 pounds each, so the five bars will weigh about 68.6 pounds. The price today is $1,115 per ounce. At today's price, the gold would be worth $1,223,000. We would have some expenses for shipping and getting the assay done. It looks like once the gold leaves here, it is out of our control. What if we were to hire a broker to sell it for us?

Chapter 49

The ad hoc committee had filed a meeting notice, and an agenda, for the gun auction and meeting the coin and currency broker at the Treasurers office. They also planned to hold the meeting in a meeting room at the Court House. The meeting had been called for 4:00 p.m. and we were right on schedule.

The Board Chairman called the meeting to order. One thing that was on the agenda was spreading Benjamin G. Mason's ashes near the den. The cremation was completed and the Sheriff had the ashes in an urn for all of us to see.

Should this be a big deal? Should we invite the news folks or should someone just go back and spread the ashes? The group thought that the latter idea was the way to go. Who would do it? The entire committee, or what?

Betty and I were asked if we would be willing to carry Benjamin's ashes and spread them. We discussed it at length and finally agreed to do it. About the only thing left to deal with is to be sure the den has the roof taken off and the cyclone fence is built around and over the remains of the den and tunnel.

Several of us on the ad hoc committee were now thinking that there may be a better, more profitable way to sell the gold. Hiring a broker was discussed. What would the commission be? We know that we paid 9% commission to sell the currency and coins. What is 9% of $1,223,000? It is $110,070. That is a big number!

Chapter 50

~~~~~

I thought the gold bar sale was set up definitely in favor of the buyer. Once we commit the gold to one of these companies, it is out of our hands. Perhaps we could do a sale, similar to when we sell our feeder calves. We deliver the feeders to a commission company that owns the sales barn. They run the sale and charge us a commission for selling the calves. They survive by getting high quality producers to bring their feeders to them and they have a good enough program to get high numbers of bidders, bidding against each other. The calves are weighed on a state inspected scale, inspected by a veterinarian, sorted by size and sex and put into the sales ring in the best way to get the highest price. Maybe we should consider doing something like that. After all, we are fairly sure the gold is worth close to $1.25 million. We have a responsibility to get the greatest price we can.

How can we do something like that? We don't even know of any place that holds that kind of auction. Besides, hauling the gold to a commission company for sale is risky. Who would do it? What provisions for protection against crooks would have to be taken?

The committee agreed that just turning the gold over to a company that buys gold is definitely giving the advantage to them. Betty said: "What about the internet? Perhaps a program like eBay would be a possibility. We advertise and ask for bids and set a closing time to accept bids. We could accept or reject any or all bids. The successful bidder would have to have a certified check sent overnight, and if we cash the check, and it is good, we ship the gold via U. S. Postal Service, registered mail with return receipt requested. If the proposed buyer did not comply, we put the gold up for sale again." We should seek some advice on how to do this.

One serious problem is that we need to get each bar assayed to determine its purity. How do we do this? Could someone come to the Treasurers Office to do it?

The ad hoc committee agreed that we should hold off on giving the Treasurer the approval to sell the gold. We were in agreement that we should at least explore selling over the internet. All agreed. The County Board Chairman will tell the Treasurer to hold off for now.

It turns out that there are several assay companies that determine the quality of many products from oil and petrochemicals to minerals and metals, to food and consumer products. I find a company with an office in St. Paul, Minnesota and they have the ability to assay gold at our site. Conversations with the firm told me that they would assay each bar, mark it with an identification mark and provide a credit card like card with the required information requested. The charge is $100 per hour, round trip from St. Paul.

Chapter 51

~~~~

The meeting adjourned and Betty and I headed for home. There were two cows that could possibly have had calves today and I had asked my grandson to check on them. They had their calves and everything seemed fine. We ate supper and since it was a very nice evening, we decided to take Benjamin's ashes back to the den and spread them.

The sun was low in the sky, so I took the flashlight just in case we had trouble. We took the four wheeler and now we can drive right up to the den. It is roped off with yellow tape, as the fence and roof work has not been done yet. It was somewhat eerie as it began to get dusk. The moon was nearly full, and was visible through the leafless trees, rising in the eastern sky.

I could hear a faint hum. Perhaps an airplane, or ultra light. Betty could hear it also. It didn't seem to come from any direction. I said, "Let's scatter the ashes and leave." I climbed up the bank and scattered the ashes around the edge of the den. All at once, Betty said, "Something just grabbed my leg!" I ran to her and saw nothing. She said it let go as I got nearer. We moved away and went to the four wheeler.

I took the flashlight and shined it toward where Betty had been standing. The leaves were moving like something was under them, moving around. It was making the leaves move in about a two square foot area. The humming was louder now, also.

That was enough for us. We got on the four wheeler and headed toward home. What the heck was back there? Neither of us believe in ghosts, but there was something unnatural about that area near the den tonight. Could someone's ghost be objecting to returning Benjamin's ashes? Why did we hear humming tonight?

We had only gone a short distance when a thought occurred to me. We stopped and walked back near the den. I shouted, "CALEB." Immediately the humming stopped and the leaves stopped moving! This was too freaky. We turned and hurried back to the four wheeler and headed home. By now we had the lights of the four wheeler on and a large owl flew right across our path about ten feet away.

That was very scary. We made it home and now question whether ghosts really do exist.

Chapter 52

~~~~~

The county forestry crew was able to complete the removal of the roof and put up the chain link fence. The ad hoc committee called a meeting for May 15th. The agenda was posted and the meeting got started at 9:00 a.m. The biggest agenda item was how are we going to proceed with the sale of the gold bars.

I told what the company that does assays had told me about the charges and information they would provide for us. We know that we need to get the bars assayed before we could offer them for sale. We agreed and voted to contact the company in St. Paul and enter into a contract with them. Corporate Council will contact them.

The question came up about contacting the Irish Charities in Hagerstown, Maryland. No one has told them anything yet. We agreed that since Benjamin wanted the gold to go to the Irish Charities and the county agreed to split it, perhaps we should see if they want the gold bars rather than half of the money from the sale of the bars. This could be another sticky wicket. First of all, how do we split a bar exactly in half. Also, we can't saw it in half as that produces gold dust which could be difficult to deal with. A large metal shear might be able to cut it in two. Gold is quite soft and very malleable, so we could cut a bar in half, if needed. The feelings of the committee was that we should contact Doctors of Mercy, the Irish Charity of Hagerstown. Tell them what has transpired and see if they want the gold or half of the proceeds from the sale of the bars. Betty volunteered to contact the Doctors of Mercy.

Betty and I told the committee of what happened when we spread Benjamin's ashes on May 11th. No one on the committee has ever heard any humming. Corporate Council has done, some research on the paranormal. He suggested that there apparently has been a great injustice done and one or more of those involved can not find peace. "It sounds very strange, I know, but that is one way those involved can show that they object to being wronged," said Corporate Council.

Apparently Caleb's spirit, or ghost, is still hanging around after at least 135 years. We wonder if Caleb's spirit is dangerous. Corporate Council said, "Maybe." Corporate Council does not plan to ever return to the den. He suggests that none of the other members of the ad hoc committee go near the den either. Betty and I are quite sure we will not go near the den again, either. We are confused on ghosts.

Betty contacted Doctors of Mercy. The contact person was flat out amazed when he heard about Benjamin and leaving the gold to Irish Charities. He also appreciated the fact that the gold belongs to the county, and was thankful the county board chose to split it evenly. He would have to get the opinion of the Doctors Board and call back. They were to meet in three days. He did agree to share in the cost of getting the gold assayed.

A contract was agreed on to assay the gold bars. The company would send someone on May 27th. It could be done in one day.

The Doctors of Mercy held their meeting, and while they were intrigued by the possible arrival of 2 ½ gold bars, they would be very happy with ½ of the proceeds of the sale of the five gold bars. Betty asked if they had any plans for its use yet. "Yes we have," was the reply. "Since it was directed to go to Irish Charities, we plan to open a storefront Doctors office in Hagerstown. There is a large percentage of people living here that are of Irish decent. We would call it 'Benjamin's Clinic'. Treatments would be free for as long as our funds hold out."

The company from St. Paul came to do the assay of the gold bars. The County Treasurer then listed them for sale on the internet with the specifications and weight of each bar. The bars were offered with an eight hour limit to place bids. All, or any, bids could be accepted or rejected.

Betty and I went to the Treasurers office to watch the bidding. It began at once. The price of gold on the Mercantile Exchange that day was $1,148 per ounce. That means that the 68.6 pounds of gold could possibly sell for $1,260,000 that day. The bars were numbered one through five. The highest bid received was posted and was the leader until another bid was higher. Since the exact weight of each bar was listed, the bid was requested in dollars, not price per ounce, as it is on the spot market. Bidders would have to calculate how much they wanted to spend on a bar. If the bid held up, and the county agreed to it, the buyer would be notified and they would need to send a certified check to arrive by overnight mail, or be hand delivered. The county could reject the highest bid for the eight hours. If that happened, bidding begins again.

The Treasurer had set the minimum bid on each bar at about $252,000. She was hoping for more, but if that was what was the high bid at the end of bidding she would accept it. The bidding started at 6:00 a.m. CDT. This means that bidding would close at 2:00 p.m. CDT.

Other information posted tells buyers that if there is a dispute about weight or purity of a bar, both parties will negotiate to resolve the dispute. Bars will be shipped by U. S. Postal Service, unless otherwise specified. Successful bidders must tell how the gold is to be shipped and send a certified check to cover shipping and whatever costs are involved to package the gold for shipping, including insurance.

The bids were very interesting to watch. All bids started a little below the minimum price. Hour by hour, the price kept rising. We could see several bidders bid on all five bars. By noon, nearly every bar was bid at $329,000, or higher. Speculation must be for gold prices to go much higher in the near future.

At 1:00 p.m., all bars are over $340,000. There are definitely less bidders compared to the early bidding. At 1:30 p.m. all bids were over $348,000. The internet announces 30 minutes left to bid and began counting down 29, 28, etc. At 1:45 p.m., all bids were over $351,000. Two new bidders had placed bids.

At 1:55 p.m. all bids were over $357,000, all by one bidder. At 1:58 p.m. a bid of $361,549 for each bar was made. Time expired so no new bids could be placed. The County Treasurer was astounded!! Should she accept the bids? By now all the other ad hoc committee members were in the office, as were others. The gold prices could continue tomorrow, but it may not. The feelings were clear. We should take the bids!!

The Treasurer announced the successful bidder was MNX Precious Metals of San Francisco, California. She sent the message that a certified check for $1,807,745 must be sent by overnight service to arrive by 2:00 p.m. the next day to complete this transaction. Just for the fun of it - if we would have hired a broker for 6% commission, we would have had to pay them $108,464. A lot of money.

MNX Precious Metals need to determine how they want the gold bars shipped. Maybe it won't be by U. S. Postal Service. They also must determine the cost of shipping and packaging and send a certified check to cover those costs. Their broker, Peter, will contact the County Treasurer to fine tune the details.

What a day! It was exciting to watch the bidding.

Once the gold is shipped, it looks like the work of the ad hoc committee will be done. Much has happened in the year since I discovered Benjamin's door in the forest.

Mysteries still remain about the bad feelings between Benjamin and Lucy's brothers. It may be something from the days they lived in Ireland. Possibly events at The Wilderness during the Civil War caused it. It could be that Benjamin and Lucy were lovers and her brothers resented Benjamin, or he had done some bad deed. At any rate, we did not resolve that problem.

The thing that is amazing is that it was a look back in time, finding Benjamin's body in the den. In fact, it was eerie. Imagine visiting someone in their grave. It must be similar to discovering mummies in the pyramids. To think that Benjamin laid there on his bed by the fireplace for at least 135 years, and then I found him.

I think Betty and I, along with our ad hoc committee, treated Benjamin G. Mason's remains with respect. It is intriguing to think he could be a very, very distant relative to me. I sure hope that what ever we saw at the den did not follow us home. Perhaps Caleb will be at rest if we don't go near him.

Recently, I have seen the tracks of a lone timber wolf that comes in the night and sits on a hill overlooking our buildings. This has happened several times in the past few weeks. I look for it during the day, but have never seen it.

This is very strange behavior for a timber wolf. The thought has crossed my mind: Did Caleb's ghost somehow overtake this wolf? If that happened, I am afraid we are not finished with Benjamin and his den.

The End

EPILOG

I hope the reader enjoyed this story. The part of how I found the den location really occurred like it was told. That exact spot with the spring and little stream does exist in the Washburn County forest. The rectangular basement hole exists where it was described also.

It is strange, but when I first saw that valley, I stood and contemplated it before I ventured down into it. It is a beautiful place. I got the idea of finding a door in the bank as I climbed up away from the little stream. Strange.

Both Betty and I, from time to time, found ourselves thinking Benjamin really existed. That is also very strange. We found ourselves wondering about his day to day things that are common place today. Like did he ever have warm water to wash with? Did he ever shave? It is hard to believe he ever had bacon and eggs for breakfast. How did he carry out daily body functions. With no store nearby, he would have lived a very Spartan life. Maybe that was it, he was a Spartan.

Why didn't he take his gold and live like a king? He must have been ashamed of stealing the gold and his penance would be to not spend it. Most of the information in the story is based on some facts. One real surprise was finding that a very, very distant relative was married to a Mason. Even more amazing is that her father was Benjamin Mason, as was her great grandfather. This was all written in my Mothers family genealogy, as were the deaths of relative soldiers in the Civil War.

Thanks for reading this book and letting your imagination take you to Benjamin's den and other places in the story. I hope you enjoyed it as much as I enjoyed writing it.